THE FAMOUS FIVE IN FANCY DRESS

THE FAMOUS FIVE are Julian, Dick, George (Georgina by rights), Anne and Timmy the dog.

The Five are enjoying a surprise holiday in Scotland when they notice another camper keeps acting most suspiciously. Can he really be involved with a gang of international spies? The Five's attempts to find out, and to foil his plans, soon lead to an unexpected and exciting adventure.

Cover illustration by Doug Post

The Famous Five in Fancy Dress

A new adventure of the
characters created by
Enid Blyton, told by Claude
Voilier, translated by
Anthea Bell

Illustrated by John Cooper

KNIGHT BOOKS
Hodder and Stoughton

Copyright © Librairie Hachette 1971
First published in France as *Les Cinq au Bal des Espions*
English language translation copyright © Hodder &
Stoughton
Ltd 1983
Illustrations copyright © Hodder & Stoughton Ltd 1983

First published in Great Britain by Knight Books 1983
Second impression 1984

British Library C.I.P.

Voilier, Claude
   The Famous Five in fancy dress.
   I. Title   II. Les Cinq au bal des espions. *English*
   843'.914[J]   'PZ7

ISBN 0-340-32813-4

Printed and bound in Great Britain for
Hodder and Stoughton Paperbacks, a
division of Hodder and Stoughton Ltd.,
Mill Road, Dunton Green, Sevenoaks,
Kent (Editorial Office: 47 Bedford
Square, London, WC1 3DP) by
Hunt Barnard Printing Ltd,
Aylesbury, Bucks.

CONTENTS

Chapter One

A CHANGE OF PLANS

'Oh, Timmy, I just can't wait! It feels like hundreds and hundreds of years since I saw the others – and now they're coming to spend the whole summer holiday at Kirrin! They'll be here any minute! I bet *you're* simply longing to see Julian, Dick and Anne again too, aren't you?'

'Woof!' replied Timmy the dog, wagging his tail as if he thoroughly agreed with his mistress.

George Kirrin and her dog Timmy were inseparable friends. George was an only child. Her real name was Georgina, but she didn't like it. She would much rather have been a boy, and she did look very boyish. George was impulsive and lively, and always full of ideas. She had so many ideas that they sometimes led her into trouble! But she had a kind heart, and she was completely straight-

A taxi came into sight at the top of the road.

'The Five are all together again!
Hurray for the holidays!'

forward and honest, so that made up for the rash way she sometimes acted without thinking first.

Timmy adored George, and she loved him back. She spent term-time away at a boarding school, so she was always glad to get home to her parents' house, Kirrin Cottage, in the holidays. At home in Kirrin, she could run wild and do as she liked most of the time. And she often had her cousins to keep her company.

They would soon be arriving now – and then what fun they would all have together! Julian was thirteen, and was the eldest of the four children. He was the most sensible of them too. Dick was eleven, the same age as George, and Anne, the youngest, was only just ten.

The four cousins, and Timmy the dog, called themselves the Five. In their holidays they quite often spent their time investigating crimes and solving fascinating mysteries. Along with playing outdoor games, that was their very favourite thing to do.

'Yes, Timmy dear,' said George, going to the garden gate, 'it can't be long before Julian and the others arrive! Their train must have come into the station about quarter of an hour ago – and then all they had to do was get into a taxi and tell the driver to take them to the village. Oh, listen! Did you hear that? Sounds to me like a car engine!'

George was quite right. A taxi had just come

into sight at the top of the hill. It drove down the dusty road, looking larger as it came closer, and stopped outside the gate. George ran to meet it, with Timmy at her heels.

'Here you are at last! The Five are all together again! Hurray for the holidays!'

A tall, fair-haired boy got out of the taxi, followed by a fair-haired girl and another boy – *he* was as dark as George herself. Julian, Dick and Anne had arrived. Julian quickly paid the taxi driver his fare. Dick and Anne were already hugging their cousin – they were so pleased to see her. As for Timmy, he was leaping about like a mad thing, quite beside himself with delight, enthusiastically licking the new arrivals.

'Oh, George, it's wonderful to see Kirrin Cottage again! The sea and the beach in the sunshine, and Kirrin Island too!' said Dick happily.

'And the best thing of all is seeing *you*, George!' added Anne, in her soft little voice. 'Now we're all four together again!'

Smiling, Julian interrupted her. 'All *five*, you mean! Watch out, Anne – George will never forgive you if you don't count Timmy too! Oh, look, here come Aunt Fanny and Uncle Quentin.'

George's parents had come out of the house to meet their nephews and niece.

'Hallo, children – did you have a good journey?'

asked Aunt Fanny, smiling. 'Hurry up and come indoors. There's a good tea waiting for you. My goodness, Anne, how you've grown!'

Even Uncle Quentin, who could never think of much to say to children, seemed pleased to see Julian, Dick and Anne. He patted them all on the back – and then went off to shut himself up in his study again!

'Good old Uncle Quentin!' Dick whispered to George. 'He's the same as ever – still wrapped up in his work and all his old books and papers! I suppose that's what comes of being a famous scientist!'

George didn't reply. She was really very fond of her father, and proud of him too – he was so clever! But she did think he was too strict at times. Uncle Quentin hated noise. It disturbed him while he was working. So when the children were at Kirrin Cottage in the holidays, he was always telling them to go and play out of doors, and saying that whatever they did they were not to disturb him. If Julian, George, Dick and Anne didn't do as he said he would tick them off – and sometimes they got punished too. That wasn't much fun!

However, as Uncle Quentin was in his study, tea was a cheerful and noisy meal. George's cousins were hungry after their train journey, and they really enjoyed the sardine sandwiches and honey sandwiches Aunt Fanny had cut for them. There was an iced sponge cake too, and some rock buns, and chocolate biscuits, with milk or lemonade to drink. After tea the children went out for a walk, and soon found their way down to the beach for the first bathe of the holidays. At last they went back to Kirrin Cottage, all talking and laughing as usual.

'And just think – there are two whole months of the holidays still to come!' cried Julian. 'George, I really do like coming to stay with you. My word – once I've got here to Kirrin, I don't see anything dragging me away again!'

But as it happened, Julian had spoken too soon. Because the Five were not going to spend the whole of their holidays at Kirrin Cottage after all!

Not that they knew that when Julian opened the garden gate. Aunt Fanny came to meet them – George was the first to see her. She seemed to have been on the watch for the children.

'Hallo – something's happened!' George told her cousins. 'I can tell from Mother's face. Oh dear, I do hope it's nothing serious!'

Aunt Fanny came to meet the Five, looking rather upset.

'Oh, children!' she exclaimed. 'I'm afraid I have some news you may not like. You're not going to spend the whole holidays here at Kirrin as we planned after all! I thought I'd better tell you that straight away, so you won't make any fuss about it at supper-time. Supper's ready now, and while we're eating it your father will tell you all about it himself, George. We haven't decided yet just what to do about you children – oh dear, it really is rather a nuisance!'

'Mother, whatever do you mean?' cried George. '*Why* can't we stay at Kirrin Cottage this year? I thought –'

'Hush! There's your father waving to us. Perhaps he's had a good idea. I know he was making a lot of telephone calls. Let's go and see what he has to say, children – and you will be sensible about it, won't you?'

Feeling worried, but also curious to know what it could all be about, the children hurried indoors, They sat down at the supper table in silence, and Uncle Quentin cleared his throat.

'Well, children – while you were out the postman came, with a special delivery letter for me,' he began. 'It means I have to change all my plans for the next few weeks! There's to be a big international scientific conference in Edinburgh – it was to have been in September, but now, for reasons I won't stop to explain, it's been put forward. The thing is that I'm taking your Aunt Fanny to Scotland with me, and George will be coming too.'

'Oh, but, Father –'

'Oh, but, Uncle Quentin –'

Uncle Quentin raised his hand, and the children kept quiet.

'Now, wait a minute! I haven't finished yet. You will *all* be coming with us. But when we get to Edinburgh our ways will part!'

The children were too surprised to say anything at first. Of course they all knew that George's father had to do a lot of travelling because of his work. Uncle Quentin went on to explain that he was going to speak about some very important research he had been doing at this scientific conference, and it would last a fortnight.

'You said our ways would part at Edinburgh,' George reminded him. 'What exactly did you mean?'

'Just be good enough to let me finish without interrupting, Georgina, and you will find out! Your mother and I will be staying in Edinburgh at the Midlothian Hotel, where a room has been booked for us. However, the question was, what about you four?'

He stopped, looking at the children, who were listening in suspense to every word he said. There was a twinkle in his eye for once!

'Well – Aunt Fanny and I will be far too busy to take care of you children! So you'll have to manage on your own.'

'You mean we're not staying at the hotel with you?' asked George, puzzled.

'No – you'll be camping out instead!'

'Camping out? In Edinburgh?' exclaimed the children in chorus. They had never been to Scotland before, but they knew Edinburgh was a big city. It was hard to see where they could camp!

'No – out in the Scottish countryside. I've been making a lot of phone calls, and I found out that there's a holiday camp especially for young people, about twenty miles from Edinburgh. And I've arranged for the four of you to spend a fortnight there.'

George immediately cried, 'What about Timmy?'

Uncle Quentin smiled – he didn't look nearly so strict then! He knew how much his daughter loved her dog.

'Don't worry,' he told her. 'They allow pets at the camp, so Timmy can go too!'

So *that* was all right! George was smiling broadly as she asked for more details about the holiday camp. Uncle Quentin told the children all he knew. They listened hard to everything he said – even Timmy seemed to be interested.

'It's on the banks of a loch, and it's run by a Mr and Mrs Arnold, who are both games teachers at schools in term-time. I gather there's a daily programme of things you can do, but it isn't compulsory, so if you prefer you can have plenty of free time to amuse yourselves, either on your own or with other young people.'

It really did sound rather fun. How the children chatted as they ate their supper!

'I expect we can bathe in the loch,' said Dick. 'A loch is the Scottish word for a lake, isn't it, Aunt Fanny?'

'And with luck there'll be canoes or rowing boats that we can take out on the water, too,' added George.

Yes, now the four cousins knew more about the change of plans for their holidays they weren't complaining at all. Aunt Fanny needn't have worried! The Five spent the next few days at Kirrin happily wondering what it would be like when they set off for their two weeks in Scotland.

Chapter Two

THE CAMP

Aunt Fanny and Uncle Quentin and the children all travelled up to Scotland by train – with Timmy too, of course. When they got on board the train at Kirrin station the kind guard, who knew George and her family very well, said they could have Timmy in the compartment with them. However, after a while they had to change to a fast express train – and the guard on that train wasn't nearly so friendly. He said that dogs had to travel in the guard's van. George felt very gloomy at being parted from her beloved dog.

'I almost wish he would bite that guard!' she said. '*Then* the man wouldn't want to keep him in his van! But of course, Timmy's much too well-behaved to bite people.'

However, Dick thought of something to take his

cousin's mind off her troubles. 'Cheer up, George!' he whispered. 'What's the betting we find an adventure waiting for us in Scotland – one of those exciting adventures we enjoy so much!'

Uncle Quentin never once looked out of the train window at the scenery they were passing. As usual, he was deep in his own thoughts and sat there reading his scientific papers. But Aunt Fanny listened to the children talking and sometimes joined in.

When they reached Edinburgh, Aunt Fanny and Uncle Quentin went off to the Midlothian Hotel. That was where most of the scientists coming to the conference were staying. The Five found their way to the bus station and caught a bus which would take them to the holiday camp for young people on the banks of a little lake called Loch Lean, about twenty miles away.

Hills began to appear soon after the bus left Edinburgh. Then the road itself got quite steep and winding, and it was very narrow in places. 'Oh dear,' said Anne. 'I wonder what would happen if we met a bus coming the other way?'

'I'm sure they plan the bus timetable so that buses don't meet on the narrow bits of road,' Julian reassured his little sister.

They got off the bus at the village of Leanhead, and saw the camp at once. It was in a big green meadow with trees growing here and there.

Among the trees stood little huts and tents, and some other buildings which looked as if they contained things like the dining-room and laundry, the showers, a reading room and games room and a snack bar, and so on.

When they arrived George and her cousins went straight to the office, and Mr and Mrs Arnold welcomed them warmly. The two teachers were both very nice – George knew that at once when they shook paws with Timmy! They took a lot of trouble to make the camp a friendly, homely place.

'You four are staying in huts,' said Mrs Arnold. 'You'll be more comfortable there than in tents.'

They were walking over the grass, and she waved to a young man, who came over and introduced himself.

'Hallo – I'm Andrew Saunders!' he said, smiling. 'I'm helping Mr and Mrs Arnold to run the camp. I'll show you where you're sleeping – come along!'

He led the way, and Julian, Dick, George and Anne followed. Andrew Saunders showed them two wooden huts standing side by side, one for the boys and one for the girls. Each was big enough for at least two people.

'Good!' cried George. 'Plenty of room for you too, Timmy!'

The children thought their first evening in the camp was a fine one. There was a supper of sausages and baked beans round the camp fire, followed by a mouth-organ competition. They soon made friends, and all the other children there took to Timmy. He solemnly shook paws all round, and looked as if he were quite happy to become the camp mascot.

When George and Anne were alone in their hut at last, George sighed contentedly.

'You know,' she said '*I* think it's really nice to go somewhere new, for a change! We shall enjoy Kirrin even more after we've spent two weeks here in Scotland. Though of course I shan't mind if Dick's prophecy comes true!'

'Prophecy?' said Anne, yawning. 'What prophecy?'

'In the train, Dick told me he had an idea we'd come across an exciting adventure of some sort while we were staying here!'

'Adventure?' said Anne in alarm. She looked scared. 'You don't mean solving a crime again, or getting mixed up in some other kind of mystery? Oh, I do hope not! I really *don't* like mysteries all that much myself! I'd rather just have a nice, quiet holiday.'

George cast her cousin a scornful glance.

'Don't be so feeble, Anne! Why do you think people call us the Famous Five? It's just *because* we like mysteries and we have exciting adventures!'

'Yes, I know,' said Anne. 'Well, I don't mind if

The two teachers were both very nice – they even shook paws with Timmy!

George hoped to come across an adventure, but Anne wanted a quiet holiday.

the adventures are exciting – so long as they're not *dangerous*!'

George sometimes felt impatient with her little cousin. She thought Anne was too timid – while Anne thought George was too much of a tomboy, and didn't stop to think before she acted. However, the two girls got on very well together. Perhaps that was because they *were* so very different!

After their long day, they soon dropped off to sleep, with Timmy at George's feet.

Next day it was a fine, sunny morning. Julian and Dick were the first to get up. They came and hammered on the girls' door.

'Wake up, lazybones! Breakfast-time!'

The camp rules said people could sit anywhere they liked at meal-times. If there wasn't room at one table, you went to find a place somewhere else. That meant everybody was always changing places and making new friends – you were next to somebody different at almost every meal, so you ended up knowing all the other young people in the camp.

At breakfast that morning the Five met some of the children they had been talking to the night before. The others at their table were called Susan, Margaret, John, Amy, James, Paul and Sandra. There were boys and girls of all ages from ten to seventeen staying at the holiday camp, and they all seemed very happy and cheerful. Yes, thought the

Five, the camp was a fine place!

'We're in luck,' said Julian. 'I think all the other children here are nice, don't you?'

'No, I don't!' said George, under her breath. 'I don't like that boy over there one bit! What a cross face he's got!'

All the others looked. George was pointing at a big boy of about seventeen. He was tall and strong and fair-haired, and he would have been very good-looking but for a bad-tempered expression which spoilt his face. He had a sulky sort of mouth and when he spoke he never looked straight at the person he was talking to.

'No, he certainly doesn't seem very friendly,' agreed Dick.

'You can't always judge by appearances,' Julian told his brother, 'but I agree with you, George: he doesn't *look* nice!'

The boy called John, who was sitting next to Anne, had heard what the cousins were saying. He leaned over and told them, in a low voice, 'You're right, no one likes that boy very much. His name is Rudy, short for Rudolph. We don't know much about him, but I'm sure he's foreign – he has a strange kind of accent. He's rather surly, and doesn't talk much or try to make friends, and he never does anything at all for anyone else. That's against the camp rules – we're all supposed to help each other! So it's not surprising that nobody here is very fond of him. I'd say the less you have to do with him the better.'

Sandra, a pretty girl with curly dark hair, joined in the conversation. 'Yes,' she said, 'Rudy is the right name for him – he *is* very rude! Just look at him now, taking the biggest piece of toast. And it strikes me there's something rather mysterious about him too.'

At the word 'mysterious' George pricked up her ears. Anne saw her face and couldn't help smiling. She guessed that her cousin's lively imagination was at work already!

For the next two days the Five were getting used to life in the young people's holiday camp. It was just the kind of thing they most enjoyed. They spent most of their time out of doors, exploring the countryside or going out on the loch, and they loved every moment of it.

Most of the other children staying there were good sports, honest and straightforward. In fact about the only odd one out was Rudy. He was very stuck-up, and wouldn't have anything to do with the younger children. He seemed to look down on people of his own age as well.

One morning they were all in the middle of a game. Rudy hadn't really wanted to play, saying it was too childish. In the end he did join in – but during the game he jostled Anne quite roughly when she got in his way by mistake.

'Here! You might watch what you're doing,' Julian told him sternly. 'And you jolly well might say sorry, too!'

Rudy's only reply was a shrug of his shoulders. Then he walked off. George was very indignant.

'What bad manners! Maybe he *is* from a foreign country, but he can speak English all right. Saying sorry wouldn't have hurt him!'

But just then Dick came running up to tell them something that made them all forget about Rudy.

'Julian! George! Anne! I've got news for you – Andrew's just told me about it. It's going to be great fun!'

'What is?' asked Julian.

'The people who run the camp are organising a big fancy dress party, and we're all to go. Isn't that fantastic?'

'A fancy dress party?' Anne sounded very interested. 'Golly – did you really say a fancy dress party? But where could they have one here?'

'It won't be here – it's being given in Edinburgh. Look, here comes Andrew. He'll tell you all about it.'

The others all went to meet Andrew Saunders. The young man was smiling broadly as he came towards them.

'Andrew, what's all this about a fancy dress party?' cried Anne. 'You're not just making it up, are you?'

'Of course not! It's perfectly true – there's to be a fancy dress party in a week's time for all of you staying in this camp, and it will be held at the Castle Hotel in Edinburgh. There'll be games and prizes, and dancing, and a competition for the best costume. There's only one first prize, of course, but there will be consolation prizes for the most elegant costume, the most original costume, the funniest costume, and so on. Well, do you like the idea?'

'Oh, yes!' cried Anne, jumping for joy.

'Woof!' Timmy agreed with her.

'I'll tell you what *I'm* going as – ' Dick began.

But Andrew interrupted him. 'Don't! The costumes are to be kept secret, so that the party will be even more fun. Everyone has to wear a mask until midnight, too. That will mean it's all even more mysterious!'

George's eyes were sparkling again at the mention of mystery! 'But how can we get hold of fancy dress costumes?' she asked.

'We'll make them ourselves,' Andrew explained. 'Using cheap curtain material, crêpe paper, silver foil and so on. Of course, anyone who would rather can hire a costume in Edinburgh. Most days I drive the camp van into Edinburgh to stock up with provisions, or else the Arnolds go, and we can give you a lift if you'd like.'

'I say – we'll have to think hard about all this!'

26

said Julian, laughing. 'But anyway, it sounds like a lot of fun!'

And the others all thought so too.

Chapter Three

A NIGHT-TIME PROWLER

The young people staying in the Loch Lean holiday camp were very excited. Over the next two days they kept gathering into groups for secret consultations. Wherever you went you could see people talking enthusiastically about their plans. The idea was to make costumes which would be quite cheap, but looked clever and amusing – and not let anyone except your best friends know what *your* costume was going to be.

In fact, the preparations were half the fun!

'I'm really looking forward to the party,' Dick told the others. 'Andrew says there are going to be coaches to take us into Edinburgh on the night of the party. We don't put on our fancy dress until we get there. Once we're in our costumes and masks, we all meet in the hotel's big ballroom to join in the games and competitions and dancing – until we unmask on the stroke of midnight!'

'I say!' said George excitedly, coming up. 'I've just had a telephone call from my parents – and they said they'd give each of us a little money to help with our costumes. Oh, I've got lots of ideas!'

'Have you really? You do surprise me, George!' said Julian, teasing her. 'I've never known you *not* have lots of ideas!'

'The only trouble is,' George went on. 'I can't take Timmy with me. Mr and Mrs Arnold say dogs aren't allowed at the party, even in fancy dress! Poor old Tim – you'll be terribly bored without me, won't you?'

'Woof,' agreed Timmy sadly.

'But it'll only be for one evening, you know,' George told him, 'so you'll just have to be good and wait here for me to come back.'

'Listen, none of this is helping us choose our costumes,' Dick grumbled. 'We really *must* decide how we're going to dress up.'

Julian said he'd already decided. 'I've always enjoyed reading *The Three Musketeers,* so I'm going to see if I can hire a musketeer's costume. And I'll make myself a moustache and pointed beard to stick on my face, and wear a sword, and I shall look very grand.'

'Well, *I'm* going to be a pirate!' said Dick. 'With

a cutlass and a big sash, and a black patch over one eye.'

'I've thought of a very simple costume,' George told her cousins. 'I'm going to the party as a cat burglar! All I need is a black jersey, a pair of black tights, a balaclava helmet and a black mask, and there I am! Have you made up *your* mind yet, Anne?'

'Yes,' said Anne, blushing slightly, because she was just a little vain. 'I want to dress up as a shepherdess, with a pretty cloak and hat and a crook with ribbons on it.'

The camp was simply buzzing for the next few days. John and Sandra and nearly all the other children staying there were busy making costumes for the fancy dress party.

The day before the party itself, Julian and Anne went to Edinburgh in the camp's van, to pick up the costumes they were hiring. Julian had rung up a shop in Edinburgh that hired out fancy dress, and ordered a musketeer costume for himself and a shepherdess costume for Anne. George, Dick and even Timmy went with them.

First they all went to see Uncle Quentin and Aunt Fanny, and had a lovely lunch at the hotel where they were staying. Then the children went to the shop hiring out costumes. Anne tried hers on.

'Yes, it does look pretty,' George told her cousin.

'But you know, there's one thing missing – if you really want to look like a shepherdess, you ought to take a few real live sheep to the party with you!'

Julian looked very dashing wearing his sword – though Dick said it would get in his way if he wanted to dance.

'I don't!' said Julian cheerfully. 'Who cares about dancing? It's the refreshments I'm interested in! If they have a cold chicken on the buffet table I could carve it with my sword!'

'In the old days musketeers didn't eat any of the refreshments at parties,' George told him. 'They had to stand on guard at the palace doors!'

'Yes – to keep out cat burglars!' said Julian.

Carrying their costumes, the children climbed the steep hill to Edinburgh Castle, and had a very interesting time looking round it. Then they went back to the place where they were to meet Andrew Saunders and the van, and they were driven back to the camp.

'Gosh, I'm absolutely worn out!' said George to Anne that evening. 'I'm sure I shall sleep like a log tonight.'

'So shall I,' said Anne, yawning. 'It's tiring walking about city streets – I feel as if my legs were worn out right up to the knees! I can't wait to go to bed.'

And no sooner had the girls slipped into their bunk beds than they fell fast asleep – with Timmy lying at his young mistress's feet, as usual. *He* had had a full, interesting day as well.

Julian and Dick were asleep too, in the hut next door. And soon the whole camp was silent. There were no boats out on the loch now, although it stayed light until quite late up in Scotland in the summer. However, at last darkness fell, and all was perfectly quiet.

Suddenly there was a sharp, cracking sound, like dry twigs cracking underfoot. It came from somewhere near the girls' hut. Timmy pricked up one ear. Anne heard it too, in her sleep, but she did her best not to wake up – she was so comfortable! Then the sound came again. It seemed louder and closer now. Anne turned over restlessly, and Timmy pricked up his other ear.

Twigs cracked in the silence of the night for the third time – so clearly that Anne at last opened her eyes. Out there someone was moving around, very carefully. The little girl listened, holding her breath. She felt uneasy, though she didn't quite know why.

Timmy was wide awake now as well. He looked at George, but when he realised that his mistress was asleep he kept quiet.

Slowly, Anne sat up in bed – and at the very same moment whoever it was outside bumped right into the hut. Anne nearly screamed. Anyone prowling about on the sly like this in the middle of the night couldn't be up to any good!

'It's a thief who's broken into the camp to steal things,' thought Anne. 'He'll creep into our hut – perhaps he'll murder us!'

Poor Anne had a timid nature, and her heart was thudding fast. But she could be brave too, however frightened she felt. When there was real danger to be faced, she could meet it calmly, as the others all knew! All the same, she didn't want to deal with this prowler on her own if she could help it. She decided to wake George.

Anne leaned forward. 'George!' she whispered. 'George!'

'Mmph?' replied George.

Anne bit her lip in annoyance. If George was going to make a lot of noise waking up, the prowler might come inside their hut just to keep her quiet!

She leaned over again and shook her cousin as gently as she could.

'George, there's somebody outside. I think it's a murderer! Wake up!'

'Mmph? What? What did you say?'

'Wake up – *please*!'

'A murderer? Nonsense! You're dreaming, Anne.'

'Ssh! Don't talk so loud. Listen!'

Sleepily, George sat up to listen, yawning widely. Being roused like this in the middle of the night made her feel very bad-tempered.

A muffled growl came from Timmy's throat and George threw back her bedclothes.

'Honestly, you keep on talking about *my* vivid imagination,' she grumbled, 'but it's simply nothing to yours! What's come over you, Anne? You must have been having a nightmare. Turn over and go back to sleep.'

All the same, George kept her voice low, as Anne had told her. And now Anne repeated, 'Ssh! Do listen!'

George listened – and the cracking sound came again! Realising that his mistress was awake now, Timmy got to his feet.

'Timmy, did you hear that, old fellow?' George whispered.

A muffled growl came from the dog's throat. George was convinced now! There really *was* somebody outside – somebody Timmy didn't much like, either.

'Yes, you're right,' she whispered quietly to Anne. 'But it's none of our business, is it? I mean, it could be anyone . . . say one of the other guests here, who couldn't sleep and thought he'd go for a walk. Or a lost dog who strayed into the camp.'

Timmy growled louder than before.

'Just look at Timmy!' Anne whispered back, anxiously. 'His hair is all standing on end. I'm *sure* there's someone about who wants to harm us!'

'Don't be silly,' said George, but she threw back her bedclothes all the same. 'Still, if you *must* worry about it, hang on a minute while I go and look!'

And before Anne could stop her, she was outside the hut. George was a brave little girl – sometimes she was rather *too* brave! – and she thought that if there really was any danger out there, then they could deal with it better if they knew just what it was.

She slipped out of the hut with as little noise as possible. She was wearing pyjamas, with nothing but slippers on her bare feet. Timmy followed her like a shadow. She had whispered to him to keep quiet. But she knew that if it was an animal who had made that cracking noise, straying round the camp, Timmy wouldn't hesitate to tackle it directly and drive it off. And if it was a human being . . . well, George felt she'd like to know whether it was just one of their friends who couldn't sleep, or some stranger up to no good!

Anne stayed behind in the hut, feeling quite as worried as before, but not daring to join her cousin. Meanwhile, George made her way carefully over the grass.

Suddenly a slight movement attracted her attention. Yes – there *was* a shadowy, human form moving about among the trees, not far from the girls' hut. It wore trousers and a T-shirt. George couldn't tell if it was a boy or a girl.

Feeling really interested now, she began following the mysterious prowler. 'I'd like to know more about this!' she said to herself.

And she had only just started following the figure among the trees, with Timmy still at her heels, when the moon came out from behind a cloud. To her surprise, George recognised Rudy!

She thought fast.

Why was he going for a walk at such a strange time? Of course, he was staying at the holiday camp too, so it wouldn't have seemed so very strange to see him if he hadn't been taking so many precautions as he moved about. It was obvious that he didn't want anyone to notice him!

More interested than ever, George decided to try to find out just what he was up to at this time of night. Without stopping to think that it might be a dangerous thing to do, she set off to follow Rudy wherever he was going.

'And whatever you do, Timmy, don't bark!' she told her dog in a whisper.

Timmy was just about to say, 'Woof!' to show that he understood – but then he remembered that he couldn't whisper like a human being. His 'Woof' would have come out much too loud! So he just nuzzled the palm of George's hand, to show her that he knew what she wanted.

Then George and Timmy began stalking Rudy. Where could he be going?

Chapter Four

SPIES AND A PLOT

Rudy looked very furtive as he walked on, but George could tell that *he* knew where he was going. And the farther he got from the camp, the more confidently he strode out. George, on the other hand, had to take extra care – because for one thing, like Rudy, she didn't want to wake people up, and for another, she didn't want Rudy himself to notice her.

Rudy skirted round the last few huts, and then set off along the path leading down to the loch.

'Surely he can't be going for a bathe at this time of night?' thought George, surprised. 'I know the air is quite warm, but the water must be freezing. I wonder what his idea is?'

They reached the loch in single file: first Rudy, then George and then Timmy. Of course, Rudy didn't know the other two were following him.

Now the path went on along the bank, beside the water. Without hesitating, Rudy turned left and went on down the path, going west.

'Gosh,' said George to herself, under her breath. 'Where on earth is he going to take me? Well, I'd better hurry if I want to find out – he's going faster now!'

Sure enough, Rudy's pace had suddenly quickened. Now that he was well away from the camp he didn't have to fear that anyone might see him – or so he thought! He walked on without taking any special precautions.

However, George couldn't do the same! If *she* walked much faster, she would run the risk of making a noise, and then Rudy might hear her. And how would she explain what she was doing out here by the loch, in just her pyjamas and slippers? No, she didn't dare walk much faster than she had been going before.

'What bad luck!' she thought to herself crossly.

It certainly didn't seem fair. Rudy obviously knew just where he was going, too – while George had to watch where she trod, and all the time she knew she mustn't lose sight of her quarry.

Then she had another piece of bad luck. The moon suddenly went behind a cloud. Now it was so dark that George could hardly see the path, and as she was keeping in the cover of the gorse bushes that grew beside it, she *did* lose sight of Rudy altogether.

As soon as she realised what had happened, she hurried along the path as fast as she could to make up for lost time, crossing her fingers and hoping that Rudy wouldn't hear her. But it was no good anyway – he seemed to have completely disappeared.

'Just my luck,' muttered George.

The brave girl stopped and listened hard. Yes, she could hear Rudy's footsteps somewhere among the trees ahead of her – but she couldn't make out just *where*. If he'd left the path itself, she was afraid she'd never catch up with him.

And then, as if he understood all about her difficulty, Timmy shot off ahead of her, sniffing the ground. George's spirits rose.

'Good boy, Timmy! Clever dog! Find Rudy, Timmy! Find him!'

Timmy went on, nose close to the ground . . . and George followed him. Five minutes later, at a spot where the path came down quite close to the water again, the dog stood still. George just had time to grab his collar and retreat into the bushes, dragging Timmy with her.

'Well *done*, Timmy. Clever boy! Ssh . . . Hallo, what's Rudy up to now?'

From the bushes where she had taken cover with her dog, George watched Rudy, who was standing on the path, holding a torch. He raised it slowly to shoulder height and waved it round in the air in a circle three times. Somewhere out on the dark loch, a light flashed in reply.

'Signals!' muttered George, in surprise. 'Goodness − it's like being in the middle of an adventure film! I wonder if they're just doing it for fun, or if there's something sinister about all this? I must say it does seem a bit suspicious! I should think those signals mean Rudy's going to meet somebody here − and if I don't much like Rudy, I don't expect I'd like his friends. I wonder if by any chance he's involved with a gang of thieves? What do *you* think, Timmy?'

Timmy just growled very quietly.

George's imagination was off at the gallop again! This lonely part of Scotland would be just the place for thieves to hide their stolen goods − and then hand them over to other criminals, who would take them out of the country and sell them. She could just imagine rough-looking men landing here from a boat, giving Rudy bags full of jewels − and Rudy, who was foreign himself, might go straight off with them and never be seen at the holiday camp again! Or would he hide them in the camp for a while, to throw the police off the track of his accomplices? If so, he didn't know it, but he'd have the Five to deal with! George held her breath as she waited to see what happened next.

A light flashed somewhere out on the dark loch.

George was sure Rudy and the man were up to something shady.

She heard the faint sound of a motor-boat's engine, coming over the loch.

'Well!' thought George. 'They've got a nerve and no mistake! The camp's not all that far off – anyone might hear them!'

But soon the engine was switched off, and there was only the faint sound of the boat slipping through the water to give it away in the silence.

The boat grounded by the bank, and Rudy went over to it.

'Is that you, Mr Malik?' he asked quietly.

'Ssh! Never mention names, boy!' replied a man's voice. 'That's an all-important security rule.'

Rudy and the man had both spoken in English, although they had quite strong foreign accents. George guessed they must come from different foreign countries, and so they were using the only language they both knew.

Suddenly she felt very uneasy, and shivered slightly. Crouching there in hiding, she dared not move at all for fear of giving herself away – and now she realised just how rash she'd been. How horrified her parents would be if they could see her!

On the other hand, she didn't really feel she had done anything wrong! And thinking how suspiciously Rudy had been behaving, and overhearing this meeting of his with the man in the boat, she felt more and more sure the two of them were up to something shady.

'Just as I thought, Rudy's a receiver of stolen goods,' she told herself. 'That's what it is, I bet!'

She was feeling rather cross about it all. She'd have to tell the police about Rudy, and then he'd probably be arrested. But he was staying in the camp with the rest of them – and somehow George didn't like the idea of acting as an informer on one of their companions.

She could only hear bits and pieces of the conversation, so she decided to try moving a little closer to the two speakers, although she was scared of giving herself away as she did so. What would happen if the pair of them found her spying on them?

However, moving very cautiously, she did manage to get closer and hide by another bush. Now she could hear every word they said.

'Oh, no! You're too far in with us to back out now,' the man called Malik was saying. 'You've accepted the offer made to you by my country's Secret Service – so I hope we can rely on you!'

'Yes, of course,' said Rudy, rather hastily. 'I never had any idea of letting you down! It'll be difficult, but I agreed to get hold of the plans for the secret rocket Professor Lancing had invented, so don't worry, I'll get them for you.'

Huddled in her new hiding-place along with Timmy, George could hardly believe her ears. She had been thinking the couple were ordinary thieves – but now she'd found out that they were mixed up in something far more serious. An international conspiracy!

With her quick mind, George realised at once that they were spies. She knew what a high reputation Professor Philip Lancing had, too. Her father had often mentioned him. And Professor Lancing was in Edinburgh at this very moment, for the scientific conference – while these spies were apparently plotting to steal the plans for his invention of a new, secret rocket!

George strained her ears to hear everything they were saying. This was something very important – and she knew that she herself could be in danger.

'These are your final instructions,' said Malik. 'You're to act tomorrow evening, during the fancy dress party. We picked you for the job just because no one is likely to suspect a seventeen-year-old from a kids' holiday camp. And things are going our way, since the party is to take place in the Castle Hotel, where Professor Lancing himself is staying. You must wait until midnight strikes. At that moment the lights will all go out, so that the young people can take their masks off before the last few games. Your own job is quite simple. You go into the Professor's room – he should be asleep by then – and get hold of his briefcase. Here's the master key which will open the Professor's door.'

'But suppose he *isn't* asleep?' objected Rudy.

'He will be! We'll see to that!' Malik assured him. 'There'll be a drug in the hot drink he has last thing at night.'

George shivered again, pressing close to Timmy. Even in the dim light, she could see Malik's nasty smile, and it made her blood run cold. She felt afraid of the man. He seemed to have thought of everything – and he meant to stop at nothing to get hold of the plans he wanted! How could she thwart this wicked plot?

Rudy was still doubtful.

'Suppose Professor Lancing hasn't got his briefcase with him?'

'Oh, he'll have it with him all right! He's a very cautious, suspicious character, and he will never trust his valuables to an hotel safe when he goes away. We're well informed about his habits! No, the Professor is never parted from his precious papers. He carries them about with him in a briefcase all the time.'

'Well, it certainly sounds as if you've prepared things for me, so perhaps it won't be as difficult as I thought,' admitted Rudy. 'I'm ready to do the job for you, Mr Malik!'

'Good. Now, once you have the briefcase in your hands you must leave the hotel fast. There'll be a black car waiting for you outside the main doorway. Its engine will be running, and you must get straight in.'

At this point Mr Malik and Rudy turned away from George and began walking back towards the boat. It looked as if their meeting was nearly over. George couldn't hear the end of the conversation. She had to stay in her hiding place – taking care not to move a single muscle.

Malik patted Rudy on the back, and then got into his boat. Rudy himself set off back along the path, the same way as he had come. George saw him pass her. Thank goodness he didn't know she was there!

Sensibly, George waited until Rudy was well out of sight before starting back to the camp herself. She was still feeling staggered by what she had just learnt. An international conspiracy! The Five had never been up against anything on quite such a large scale before!

'I must hurry up and tell Dick, Julian and Anne,' said George to herself, walking faster. 'And then we'll all hold a council and decide on the best thing to do. My word – what an adventure, Timmy dear!'

Though of course George knew it was all very serious, she couldn't help being a bit excited too. She did love an adventure! And it was nice to think of frustrating the plans of a gang of international spies. The thought of possible risks didn't even enter the brave girl's mind.

When she got back to the camp she hurried into the hut she shared with Anne. Anne was waiting in a state of near-panic. She jumped when George came in, and only just stopped herself screaming in alarm.

'Oh, George, it's you!' she gasped, relieved. 'You've been so long! What happened? Did you –'

'Ssh – I'll explain later,' George interrupted. 'But I must wake the boys first. Come on, Anne, come and help!'

Puzzled, Anne did as her cousin said. It took them some time and a lot of knocking to wake Julian and Dick, but at last the girls managed to rouse them.

'Golly – is it tomorrow already?' grumbled Dick, rubbing his eyes.

'Shut up!' said George impatiently, in a low voice. 'Everyone listen to me!'

By now the Five were all wide awake, and they held a council in the boys' hut. Julian, Dick and Anne listened spellbound as George described her exciting expedition. Timmy sat and looked as if *he* were listening too – although he had been with her!

'Goodness!' exclaimed Julian, when George had finished. 'So it looks as if Rudy is in the pay of a foreign power – some country that wants to get hold of the plans for that rocket.'

'Yes,' said George. 'And it's our duty to foil the plot!'

'You bet it is!' Dick agreed warmly. 'I know Professor Lancing's plans are supposed to be very valuable – *and* he's a friend of Uncle Quentin's!'

'But what can we do?' asked Anne. 'If we go straight to the police and tell them about Rudy he'll just deny it all. And it's only George's word against his! As for this Mr Malik, we don't know just who he is and we've no idea where to find him. We're only children – nobody will believe us!'

'You know, Anne's right,' said Julian. 'We need to tell a grown-up – someone the police will be more likely to believe! Then, with the information we can give them, they'll be able to catch the spies red-handed – or *black*–handed if the plans are written in ink!'

'Oh, dear. I suppose I agree, Ju,' said George, sighing gloomily. 'It looks to me as if we'd better tell my father and get *him* to warn the police, though I'd much rather have dealt with the spies on my own – well, *our* own, I mean! It would have been so thrilling, wouldn't it?'

The children talked it over for quite a long time, but in the end they all agreed that the best thing would be to tell Uncle Quentin all about it. Then *he* could warn Professor Lancing of the conspiracy, and the two scientists could go to the police and make sure the spies were arrested just as they were trying to steal the plans.

'We'll ring Uncle Quentin up in Edinburgh

tomorrow morning,' Julian said at last. 'All right, everyone? Good – so now let's try to get a little more sleep. It must be nearly morning!'

So the Five went back to bed.

However, the exciting and alarming events of the night were not over yet! Julian, Dick, George and Anne had only just dropped off to sleep when they were abruptly woken again, by shouts and terrified screams.

'Fire! Fire!'

Chapter Five

THE FIRE

'Quick! Get up, everyone!'

George and Anne were out of bed in a flash, running out of their hut to join Julian and Dick. The boys were outside already. Everything in the camp was bustle and confusion!

'Look!' cried Dick.

'Woof! Woof!' barked Timmy, very excited.

Anne turned to look the way Dick was pointing, and gave a cry of horror. Flames and thick smoke were rising from the far side of the camp.

'Yes, it's a fire all right!' cried Julian. 'How awful!'

'We'd better go and see if we can help,' said George.

The huts where the Five slept were the farthest of all from the middle of the camp. They soon saw

51

that most of the other children were already up, running to the scene of the disaster. They hurried after them.

'Oh, my goodness!' cried Anne. 'The flames are close to John's tent!'

'Let's hope the firemen get here quickly,' said Julian.

The Five soon reached the spot, and stopped in horror at the sight that met their eyes. Three wooden huts and a tent were on fire. Andrew Saunders and a team of young people were at work. Mr and Mrs Arnold had organised them into a chain, and buckets of water were being passed from hand to hand. Without a moment's hesitation, the children took their places in the chain.

'Keep going!' cried Mr Arnold. 'The main thing is to make sure the fire doesn't spread – we must keep it under control until the fire engine arrives!'

Red flames were dancing in the dim light. For a little while it looked as if so much water had been thrown on them that they were dying down – but then, unfortunately, a gust of wind blew a few sparks over to another hut, and that hut flared up too.

Sandra screamed.

'Oh no! My little brother Patrick – he's in there!'

The hut, which was made of rough pine logs, was already ablaze. Feeling terribly upset, Anne burst

As the red flames danced in the dim light the young people passed buckets of water from hand to hand.

into tears. So did Sandra. But Andrew, Julian, Dick and George moved into action! They started flinging buckets of water on the new fire as fast as they possibly could, but it was no use. The hut went on burning.

It was dreadful to think of little Patrick inside! Mr Arnold, who had been directing the people fighting the first fire, came striding over. 'What's all this? Is there still a child in there? But I said everyone in the huts nearby was to move out!'

'It's my fault!' confessed Sandra, in tears. 'Patrick's had a cold, and it seemed such a shame to wake him – so I let him go on sleeping!'

George didn't wait to hear any more. The firemen were such a long time coming, and the hut was blazing merrily! It was already impossible to reach the door and the two side windows – but perhaps if she went round to the back ... ? Without another word, George ran round the burning hut. Yes, she had guessed right! The wind, blowing from behind the hut, was beating the flames forwards, so the back of the hut was not on fire yet, though thick smoke was already pouring out of the one little window in the back wall.

However, that was the only possible way to get the little boy out!

George didn't hesitate. She jumped nimbly – but her fingers only just touched the window-sill. It was too high up for someone of her size to reach it.

But George kept her head. 'Timmy!' she called. 'Quick, come here! Now, don't move. Stay, Timmy – stay!'

She made Timmy stand under the window, and used him as a kind of stepping-stone. The good dog stood there firmly, bracing himself on all four paws to keep his back steady. Now George could get hold of the window-sill. She hauled herself up, and dropped down inside the hut.

Smoke came billowing to meet her. George felt it getting into her nose, throat and lungs. Luckily she had a handkerchief in her pyjama pocket. Both handkerchief and pyjamas were very damp from water that had sloshed out of the buckets being passed from hand to hand. There was just a chance . . .

Quickly, George got the hanky out and tied it over her nose and mouth. Then she made for the bed. The flames had not reached it yet, and a slight little figure lay there. Patrick!

Half-suffocated already, the little boy was lying unconscious at the mercy of the fire, which was crackling and hissing quite close to him now. George grabbed him, picked him up, and with some difficulty dragged him over to the window. But once there she stopped, suddenly panic-stricken. There wasn't time to go back and look for a chair, and she was not strong enough to lift the little boy out of the window – what was more, she was struggling for breath herself.

What could she do? What would become of them now?

Then the brave little girl heard someone shouting outside. 'George! Hang on, George! We're here!'

A ladder was put up to the window, and Andrew's head appeared at the top of it. The young man leaned into the hut.

'Quick, George – hand me Patrick!'

With a tremendous effort, George managed to lift the little boy, and Andrew grabbed him by his pyjamas.

For a few seconds poor George thought she herself was done for. The flames were coming closer, and she could hardly breathe! Then Andrew's head and shoulders reappeared, and he leaned in again.

'Your turn, George – here, hold out your wrists! Quick!'

She obeyed, feeling quite dazed, and felt Andrew grasp her wrists and haul her up. Then she fainted!

When George came round, she was lying on the grass with her cousins standing anxiously around her. Anne's eyes were red, and Julian and Dick looked as if they might have been crying just a little too!

'Andrew saved your life, George,' Julian told

her, 'But *you* rescued Patrick! By the way, he's quite all right.'

'But how did anyone guess I was in there?' stammered George, sitting up. 'My lungs were so full of smoke I wasn't even able to call for help!'

'Timmy came running to find us,' Anne explained. 'He led us to the window, stood there and barked – so as you can imagine, it didn't take us long to work out what he meant!'

'Dear old Timmy! You saved my life!'

Timmy was delighted to see that his mistress was conscious again. He celebrated by licking her face enthusiastically all over! As for Sandra, she came running over and hugged George hard.

'My little brother would be dead but for you!' she cried. 'And now he's going to be all right. The firemen gave him first-aid. Look – they're getting the better of the fire. I think the danger will be over soon!'

Suddenly George felt fine again herself. How glad she was she had managed to save Patrick!

She got up and went to find Andrew and thank him. Now that the firemen had arrived to take over, he was having a moment's rest, mopping his forehead.

'George, you were really very brave!' the young man said when he saw her.

'Well, so were you! But for you –'

'Never mind that!' said Andrew. 'Now, children,

you must go and get dry and put some clothes on. We're *all* drenched. It's broad daylight now, and it isn't worth trying to get back to sleep, so suppose we meet in the dining-room in fifteen minutes' time? A good breakfast will make us all feel better!'

The Five all agreed.

'Yes!'

'Good idea!'

'Right!'

'See you in a minute!'

'Woof! Woof!'

They hurried back to their own huts. 'You know what!' said Julian suddenly. 'We were going to telephone Uncle Quentin first thing this morning – and what with all the excitement of the fire we haven't done it yet.'

'There's plenty of time!' replied George, and she added, 'You know, I'm really feeling rather pleased with myself!'

Now it wasn't at all like George to be boastful, and Dick looked at his cousin in surprise. 'Why?' he asked. 'Because you rescued Patrick from the fire?'

George roared with laughter.

'Goodness me, no! Because the Arnolds have just told me Timmy can have a reward for what *he* did today! As a special treat, they'll let him come to the fancy dress party with us!'

Anne looked pleased and surprised. 'You mean

he can come to the Castle Hotel this evening?'

'Yes, that's right. And you must admit he deserves a treat! I've had a good idea, too – he can be part of *your* fancy dress, Anne! You're going as a shepherdess, and Timmy can be your sheepdog! He'll make up for your not having any real sheep!'

The children began to laugh – and Timmy, guessing they were talking about him, barked happily as he chased along the path.

A little later they met their friends again at breakfast. As soon as Patrick saw George, he flung his arms round her neck, and insisted on sitting next to her. He was a dear little boy, fair-haired and full of fun – usually he was laughing all the time, but now he seemed rather upset. George was sorry.

'The fire must have been a dreadful shock to him,' she whispered to Sandra. 'He doesn't seem his usual self at all!'

'Well – he *has* had a shock, but it's not what you think!' Sandra told her, with a little smile. 'Poor Patrick is feeling cross because he's lost his fancy dress for the party! He was going as a clown, but his clown costume was burnt.'

'Oh dear – poor little boy!' said Anne sympathetically. 'What can we do to cheer him up?'

Dick had an idea. 'Since Patrick's lost his costume in the fire, why don't we make him a new one?' he suggested. 'It can't be all that difficult!'

'Yes, let's!' cried George enthusiastically. 'I know – John has a mask with a monkey's face! He isn't using it himself, so that would do for Patrick's mask. And for the rest of the costume, all he needs is an old coat, and we'll sew or stick some nice white feathers on it!'

'What's he supposed to *be*, though, poor little thing?' asked Julian, amused.

'Why, the Abominable Snowman, of course!'

Everyone burst out laughing – even Patrick, and he wouldn't be satisfied until John had gone off to fetch him his monkey mask. After breakfast, Sandra and Anne unstitched an old sleeping bag and got out the light, downy feathers inside to stick them on Patrick's coat.

George suddenly remembered that it really was time to telephone her parents at their hotel, and tell her father what she had heard that night.

'Why don't you come too?' she said to Julian and Dick.

So the three cousins went off to the building where the camp's office was. There was a telephone outside the office. But they were delayed on their way there!

Several reporters from the newspapers, who had heard about the fire at the holiday camp, had just arrived, and they surrounded the three children. 'You must be Georgina Kirrin, little girl, aren't you? Mr Arnold told us how you saved a child's life! Right – now we'd like a few photographs!'

Lights flashed!

'I say – your picture will be in all the papers this evening, George, old thing!' said Dick, just a little enviously.

But George herself hated having a fuss made of what she'd done. She refused to pose for any photographs except with Timmy by her side – she thought her dog ought to get *his* full share of the credit!

By the time the reporters let the children go it was nearly eleven o'clock. George hurried to the telephone, and her cousins watched as she dialled the number of her parents' hotel. However, she hung up again almost at once, looking downcast.

'I shan't be able to get hold of my mother and father at all today!' she told the boys. 'Apparently they left the hotel an hour ago to go on an excursion – and they won't be back till late tonight! By that time, Rudy will have had his chance to steal the Professor's plans.'

'Oh, what bad luck!' said Julian, frowning. 'What shall we do now?'

'Why – manage on our own, of course!' said George, suddenly cheering up. She was full of energy again. 'It won't be the first time the Five have done that! We don't really need my father, do we? I mean, we're going to be at the hotel where

Professor Lancing is staying ourselves, and we'll be on the spot to warn him what the spies intend to do!'

'But suppose he's already been drugged by the time we reach the hotel?' Dick objected.

'In that case we'll have to guard his precious plans ourselves!' said George at once.

Chapter Six

IN THE CASTLE HOTEL

The rest of the day was all hurry and bustle – the whole camp seemed to be turned upside down! Because of the fire, the Arnolds had to put the children from damaged huts to sleep with other people. Sandra and Patrick's hut had been completely destroyed, so George and Anne said that Sandra could share theirs, and Patrick was to go in with Julian and Dick.

Of course the fire meant a lot of worries for the Arnolds and Andrew Saunders – but they didn't want the children to be affected any more than was necessary, so the fancy dress party was going ahead just as it had been planned. Soon all the children were busy, happily putting the finishing touches to their costumes. They had been looking forward to the party for so long!

Every hut and tent turned into a changing room – and was out of bounds to everyone except its occupants. It really was rather difficult trying to keep the secret of your costume from everyone but your closest friends! There were bursts of laughter to be heard all over the camp that day.

'There!' said Dick triumphantly, showing off his fancy dress to Julian and Patrick. 'How do you like my pirate outfit? Don't you think I look fierce?'

He was really laughing at himself, but little Patrick *did* seem to be very impressed by the black patch Dick was wearing over his left eye.

'Yes, Dick, and why don't we saw off one of your legs and give you a wooden pegleg instead? You'd look even more piratical then!' said Julian.

'So he would,' Patrick agreed, seriously, 'but you know, Julian, he wouldn't be able to dance or play games very well with a pegleg!'

The girls were trying on their own costumes too. It was great fun. Sandra was going as the Fairy Queen, and was practising draping herself in the gauzy veils she would be wearing. Anne, biting her lip with concentration, was busy cutting out a gold cardboard star to go on the end of Sandra's magic wand. George wasn't interested in anything as childish as fairies and magic wands! She smiled, knowing *she* didn't have to try anything on. Her cat burglar's costume couldn't have been simpler, and it was a perfect fit.

The fun of getting ready for the fancy dress party almost made the four cousins forget about the threat hanging over Professor Lancing. They had quite made up their minds to foil the spies' plot – but as there was nothing they could do about it just yet, they were enjoying the happy atmosphere all around them.

The children had a rather late tea at the camp, to keep them going until it was time for the buffet supper at the party, and as soon as tea was over they went off to their huts or tents, laughing and talking cheerfully, to fetch the cardboard boxes containing their costumes and masks. And a little later they were boarding the two coaches that had come to drive them into Edinburgh.

The drive was an uneventful one. They went along the winding road from the loch, and then reached the wider roads close to Edinburgh. However, as they got closer to the city Julian, George, Dick and Anne began to feel a little anxious. They were wondering whether they would be able to get in touch with Professor Lancing before the cowardly spies who had designs on his plans had drugged him.

'And I only hope he'll agree to listen to us,' thought George, watching the landscape go past the coach windows. 'It *is* rather a pity my mother and father aren't available, after all – he'd have been a lot more likely to take notice of *them*!'

The coaches stopped outside the big double doors of the Castle Hotel. The children all got out. They were rather quiet as they walked into the hotel – it was such a grand, luxurious place! But a friendly, smiling receptionist came to meet them and welcome them.

'This way, please, ladies and gentlemen!' she said.

She showed the girls into one big changing room and the boys into another. The rooms were divided up by screens into little cubicles, and there wasn't much light until the children had found their way into separate cubicles – then the main lights were switched on! Now all they had to do was change into their costumes and come down to the big ballroom, their faces hidden by masks.

The friendly receptionist showed them the way to go, and soon the huge ballroom was full of cheerful party guests. What fun it was, walking around in costume and trying to guess who was who in the colourful crowd!

A little group soon gathered in one corner of the room – and you didn't have to be a genius to guess that its members were Julian, Dick, George and Anne, in their costumes. The fact that Timmy was with them – pretending to be Anne's sheepdog, of course – was enough to give them away!

'Right!' said George. 'Now we're here we'd better hurry up and find Professor Lancing. Let's go to the reception desk and ask for him. Every second counts now! Follow me!'

And leaving the others to enjoy the lavish refreshments laid out on long tables, or play the games which were already in full swing, the Five went off to the hotel's reception desk.

There was a man sitting behind the desk. He smiled in a friendly way when he saw them coming.

'Please, sir,' said Julian politely, taking off his plumed musketeer's hat, 'do you know if Professor Lancing happens to be in his room at the moment?'

'Yes, he is,' said the man, glancing at a board where a lot of keys were hanging. 'If he were out his key would be here, but it isn't.'

'In that case,' said George, 'would you tell him that Quentin Kirrin's daughter wants to speak to him, and it's urgent? I'm sure he'll agree to see me – at least, I do hope he will!'

Rather surprised by the little 'cat burglar's' serious tone of voice, the man lifted his telephone and pressed a switch on the switchboard. He was calling Room 123. But after a moment he hung up, looking a little surprised.

'That's odd,' he said. 'I'm sure Professor Lancing *is* in his room, but no one's answering the phone. Well, I suppose the Professor doesn't want to be disturbed. I'm very sorry to disappoint you, Miss Kirrin, but I can't go on ringing – it would annoy him. Why don't you try again tomorrow morning?'

George nodded, as if she thought that was a good idea. She thanked the man, and then hurried off, followed by her cousins.

'Did you hear that?' she whispered. 'The Professor's in his room, but he isn't answering the telephone!'

'So he must be drugged already!' Dick deduced.

'Yes, that's what I think, too,' said Julian, frowning.

'Oh dear – what shall we do?' said Anne. She sounded scared.

'We must act fast! There's no time to lose,' said George firmly. 'As my father isn't here, and the Professor himself has been drugged and can't defend himself, it's up to us to save the situation. We *must* make sure the plans for that new rocket don't fall into another country's hands!'

'Countries don't have any hands,' Dick pointed out.

'Idiot! I meant the spies' hands, of course!'

'Don't quarrel, you two,' Julian told them. 'Time's passing – and Rudy is going to act at midnight, don't forget.'

'Why is he waiting until midnight?' asked Anne, shivering slightly.

'Because that's when all the lights go out and we all take our masks off,' George patiently explained.

The man tried to contact Professor Lancing in his hotel room.

George disappeared – a slim black shape running upstairs.

'Oh – so you mean Rudy will take advantage of the darkness and confusion to slip away without being seen?' said Anne. 'Yes, I see – no one will even notice he's gone! And he can get straight into the Professor's room with the master-key Malik gave him, and steal the briefcase!'

'Well, he can't, because we're going to get hold of the briefcase first!' George told her cousin. 'Now, let's start by going to see if Professor Lancing's door is locked. If by any chance he left it open, everything will be much easier! We only have to march in, get there well ahead of Rudy, and take the briefcase away for safe keeping.'

'Well – which of us is going up to the Professor's room, then?' asked Dick, trying not to sound as if he'd love to have that bit of the adventure for himself. Of course, he was longing to go!

'You are, Dick! Four of us would attract too much attention,' George told him. 'And if anyone catches you trying the door handle, you'll just have to think of some excuse – anything! For instance, you could say you thought it was the bathroom door. And you'd better take that black patch off, and leave your cutlass here – then you won't look so noticeable!'

'Hold on – just where *is* Room 123?' asked Dick, getting rather bewildered by all George's instructions.

'On the first floor, of course – you can tell

70

because the first number is 1. It'll be the twenty-third room on the first floor.'

'Oh, I see. All right, I'm off!'

Dick ran upstairs – he preferred running to using the lift – and Julian, George and Anne waited in the hotel lobby, in the shelter of a screen with pot plants climbing all over it. They were hoping against hope that their luck would be in!

Dick seemed to be gone a long time, but at last he reappeared, looking rather downcast – and empty-handed.

'I'm afraid the Professor's door *is* locked,' he told the others. 'I tried the handle several times, but it wouldn't budge. Then I knocked – really loud, and I even called to the Professor in a low voice, but there wasn't any reply, so I listened at the keyhole and I could hear snoring. I saw light under the door too.'

'Oh dear! I suppose they made sure the Professor had a strong sleeping pill, and he'll be under the effect of it for hours,' sighed Anne.

Julian looked at his watch. 'Well, we must do something!' he said. 'It's eleven o'clock already.'

'Yes, and Sandra and Patrick must be wondering where we are,' added George.

'Do something?' said Dick to his brother. 'Yes, fine – but do *what*? *We* haven't got a master-key to open doors for us!'

'No – but we can always use our brains instead,

can't we?' replied George, rather impatiently. 'Since the door is locked, we'll have to get in through the window! There's a ledge running round the outside of the hotel at the level of the first-floor windows – I saw it as we were arriving. And it's so warm today that I'm sure the windows will be open.'

'Oh, George, we can't scramble all the way up there!' cried Anne. 'It would be terribly dangerous – and I get dizzy very easily.'

'People outside the hotel would see us, too,' Julian pointed out. He didn't sound very keen on George's idea.

'No, it wouldn't be dangerous!' said George. 'Not for me – *I* never get dizzy!' Her cousins were looking at her blankly, so she added, 'You see, there's no point in all four of us trying it. I'll go on my own. Remember, the Professor's room is only on the first floor. So even if I did fall I wouldn't kill myself – at least, I don't think so! As for being seen from outside the hotel – well, I've got one big advantage there! I'm dressed up as a cat burglar already, in black, and it's nearly dark now. I couldn't have chosen a better costume. I'm not likely to be spotted at all!'

'But how will you get on the ledge in the first place?' asked the practical Dick.

'Easy!' said George. 'I'll climb out of the little window of one of the first-floor bathrooms and get

72

on the ledge like that. Then I'll make my way along it. The trickiest bit will be finding which room is the Professor's, but I expect I'll be able to look in and see the Professor himself asleep. It's lucky he didn't put the light out before the drug took effect on him.'

'But suppose you land in somebody else's room by mistake?' asked Julian, frowning.

'Don't worry! I won't! I know what Professor Lancing looks like – I've seen lots of photographs of him in the scientific magazines my father reads.'

George had an answer for everything – and as time was slipping by fast, her cousins let her have her way. Even Julian realised it was probably the best thing to do.

'Just give me a few minutes' start,' she said. 'After that, *you* come upstairs and wait in the corridor outside the Professor's room – only of course you mustn't *look* as if you're waiting there! I'll open his door from the inside to let you in. Timmy, stay! Be a good boy. Hang on to him, Julian, just to make sure he doesn't follow me – I don't see dear old Timmy as a cat burglar!'

And George disappeared – a slim black shape running upstairs to the first floor. Her cousins waited for a while, feeling rather anxious. George was so daring! They would have liked to go out into the street to make sure she was all right when she reached the ledge, but of course they couldn't do that without spoiling their whole plan.

At last Julian moved. 'Come on!' he said. 'I think it's time to go up now.'

And a musketeer, a pirate, a shepherdess and a sheepdog climbed the stairs in single file! What would they find at the top?

Chapter Seven

MIDNIGHT STRIKES

Luckily, what with the party going full swing in the hotel ballroom, there were not many people coming and going in the rest of the building. Once Anne and her brothers got up to the first-floor landing they were relieved to see that they were quite alone there.

'This one's Room 123!' whispered Dick, pointing to Professor Lancing's door.

Meanwhile, George was carrying out her bold plan. She had climbed through a bathroom window, and found herself out on the ledge running all along the outside wall. It was in deep shadow. She didn't look down as she groped her way along the narrow ledge, pressing close to the dark wall. She was quite invisible from the street.

Twice, she had to pass a lighted window. She

did so very carefully making sure they were neither of them the window she was looking for, and then going on in silence.

And at last George's daring was rewarded! She came to the third lighted window. Craning her neck, she glanced at the room inside, and then smiled under her mask.

'Good – I've found Professor Lancing's room! Here goes!' she murmured to herself.

She jumped nimbly down into the room. Once inside she didn't even stop to get her breath back, but quickly pulled the thick velvet curtains to hide the window.

'Phew!' she sighed.

Then she tiptoed over to Professor Lancing. The scientist was lying on his bed, fully dressed and sleeping like a child. A loud, unmusical snore escaped him now and then – and whenever he snored his heavy breathing made his moustache quiver. George could hardly help laughing. You would never have known this fat, funny-looking man was one of the greatest, most famous scientists in the whole world!

But George didn't waste any more time looking at the Professor. She hurried to open the door to her cousins.

'Well done, George! You did it!' said Anne admiringly.

'No, as a matter of fact I didn't!' George teased

her. 'I actually broke my neck falling off that ledge, and this is my ghost talking to you!'

'When you've *quite* finished talking rot . . .' said Dick, nervously looking over his shoulder. 'Come on – we'd be in a nice mess if anyone came along and saw us standing here!'

'Well, come inside, then!' George told him.

Julian turned to his little sister. 'Anne, I think you'd better stay here in the corridor with Timmy, to keep watch. If you see anyone coming, just whistle!'

'But I can't whistle!' Anne objected.

'Well, sing, then!'

'Sing what?'

'Oh – well, Little Bo-peep, for instance!'

'All right. That would certainly suit my costume!'

'And if the person you see coming is Rudy, blow your nose – very loud! Right! It's getting close to midnight now . . .'

Leaving Anne and Timmy on guard in the corridor, the boys went into the Professor's bedroom with George. They carefully closed and locked the door after them.

'Now what?' whispered Dick.

'Now let's look inside the briefcase,' said George.

Julian found the leather briefcase almost at once. Of course, the Professor had had no idea he

The scientist snored contentedly as the children wondered what to do with his papers.

was going to fall asleep so suddenly, so it was simply lying on his bedside table, where he had put it down.

Julian stopped and wondered what to do. 'You see, if we just take this briefcase away with us,' he pointed out, 'the spies may spot us with it, recognise it and snatch it away! On the other hand, we can't leave it here – that would spoil everything!'

'Here, let me have it!' said George. 'I've had an idea!'

She took the briefcase from Julian, opened it, and took out a pile of carefully numbered sheets of paper covered with writing, figures and diagrams.

'Gosh – those must be the plans for the secret rocket!' murmured Dick, rather awestruck.

'George, what on earth are you doing?' asked Julian in alarm.

'Never mind – just help me! You too, Dick! Quick – get hold of the Professor's shoulders and lift him up for a minute.'

'But what's the idea?'

'There isn't time to explain now!' said George. 'Oh, *do* hurry up!'

So the boys did as she asked, without really understanding why. They took hold of the Professor's shoulders and lifted his top half. It was quite difficult, because he was so heavy.

George immediately slipped the notes underneath the bedspread on which he had been lying, spreading them out flat. 'There!' she said, pleased. 'Now, put the Professor back just where he was. Quick – midnight will soon be striking!'

'All right, Cinderella!' Dick teased her.

The boys laid the Professor gently back on top of the bedspread – and on top of the plans for his rocket! He began noisily and contentedly snoring again. The children couldn't help smiling.

'Poor Professor! He's got no idea what a lot of trouble he's giving us!' said George. She looked round. 'Now – I bet there are some newspapers or magazines in this room somewhere.'

'Yes, over there – look. A whole pile of magazines. But what do you want them for?' asked Julian, interested.

George picked up some of the magazines and began stuffing them into the Professor's briefcase. As she did so, she explained.

'Well, we don't want to disappoint our dear friend Rudy, do we? He'll be coming up on purpose to get hold of this briefcase – so we'll let him have it! Then Mr Malik can't say he didn't do the job properly! Of course, he'll change his tune when the briefcase is actually opened – but we won't be there to hear what he says to Rudy then! To tell you the truth, I'm a bit sorry about that!'

Dick began to laugh. 'Honestly, George! I can just imagine their faces when they find they haven't got the precious plans after all, only some old magazines!'

'That's just too bad for them!' said George, closing the briefcase. 'It will serve them right!'

'I can tell you someone else who'll be as baffled as the spies!' said Julian, smiling with amusement. 'I wonder what Professor Lancing is going to think when he wakes up, to find that his briefcase has gone – '

'And that he's been lying there, snoring, on top of his notes and diagrams!' added Dick.

George didn't have time to reply. Somewhere out in the city, a clock began slowly striking twelve. The big moment had come!

'Midnight!' cried Dick. 'Come along, we'd better get out! Rudy will be here any moment now.'

George quickly put the briefcase back on the bedside table and followed her cousins to the door.

*   *   *

Downstairs in the ballroom, everyone was laughing and shouting. The lights had just gone out! Little Patrick, dressed up as the Abominable Snowman, squeezed his sister's hand.

'Sandra, I'm scared!' he whispered.

'There's nothing to be scared of,' she told him. 'This is when we all take our masks off.'

'But it's so dark – I can hardly see a thing!'

'It won't be dark for long, only five minutes! After that they'll turn the lights on again so that we can all recognise each other.'

Laughing groups were already trying to make out each other's faces in the dim light. All the masks were off now, and people were looking round for their friends. Sandra was about to help Patrick off with his monkey mask – but in all the confusion, she somehow got separated from him. Frightened, little Patrick began searching for her.

'Sandra! Sandra!' he called.

But other people were talking in loud voices – there was an awful lot of noise. The poor little boy, panic-stricken, suddenly saw the lighted doorway into the hotel lobby and hurried towards it.

Meanwhile, on the first stroke of midnight, Rudy had gone into action. All through the evening he had kept well out of the way, waiting patiently. He had on the sort of big cloak, called a domino, that people sometimes wear to hide a fancy dress costume. Malik had got hold of it for him. And underneath he was dressed like an hotel waiter in black trousers, a striped waistcoat, and soft shoes. It was an ideal costume to wear if you wanted to walk about in an hotel without attracting attention!

As soon as the lights went out, Rudy took off his domino and the black velvet mask hiding his face, and hurried out of the ballroom. Nimble as a cat, he ran straight upstairs to the first floor.

Hearing the laughter and noise down below, Anne knew the dangerous moment had come. The hotel clock was striking twelve too. The little girl couldn't help shivering.

'Oh, Timmy!' she murmured. 'I do wish Julian and the others would hurry up!'

The sudden sound of light footsteps on the stairs made her turn her head. Whoever it was running upstairs came out on the landing – and the little shepherdess recognised Rudy! She turned quite pale, while her 'sheepdog', hair standing on end, growled in a low tone.

'It's Rudy!' she gasped.

Then, pulling herself together, she remembered Julian's instructions and began to blow her nose very hard.

George and the boys heard Anne's warning from inside the bedroom, where Professor Lancing was still sleeping peacefully. They had been on their way to the door, but they stopped and stood perfectly still, ears straining to hear the sounds in the corridor.

Anne blew her nose again. This time she managed to make her signal sound really urgent! When the three cousins heard it they reacted very fast, but very quietly. Without even stopping to consult each other, they made their way into the private bathroom next to the bedroom, and Dick closed the door behind them.

'No, Dick – leave it open a little!' George whispered to him. 'Then we can see what's going on inside the room.'

Meanwhile, out in the corridor, Anne was doing her best to delay Rudy. He had seen her as soon as he came upstairs, and he was very annoyed, because he had expected to be quite alone on the landing. However, he turned his head aside and went towards a broom cupboard, hoping she hadn't recognised him.

Anne really did very well indeed! She not only pretended she *hadn't* recognised Rudy, she acted as if she wasn't a bit interested in the 'waiter'. Stooping down, she pretended to be searching hard for something.

'I wonder if I could have dropped it here?' she asked Timmy, in a low voice. 'Oh, yes – here's my comb at last! I'm so glad I've found it!'

And she pretended to be picking something up. Then she hurried off to the lift, along with Timmy.

As soon as she had pressed the ground floor button and gone down, Rudy, who had been watching her out of the corner of his eye, made up for lost time. He hurried to the door marked 123, took the master-key out of his pocket, put it in the lock and turned it. The door opened.

From the bathroom where they were hiding,

Julian, Dick and George saw the 'waiter' slip into the room.

'There's Rudy!' whispered Julian.

'Bother him!' said Dick.

Once inside the room, Rudy immediately locked the door again and then looked round. He saw – and heard – Professor Lancing, and smiled.

'Was there anything else you required, sir?' he murmured mockingly, in the voice of a well-trained waiter. 'You might make less noise if you put something over your nose, sir!'

But the young foreigner's bright eyes had caught sight of the black leather briefcase on the bedside table.

'Dear me,' he went on sarcastically, 'how very untidy of you, sir! You really ought to take more care of your things, sir – fancy leaving such valuable documents lying about! What can you have been thinking of, sir?'

He picked up the briefcase. It looked as if he was going to open it – Julian and Dick were in suspense. What would happen if Rudy found the worthless magazines now?

But George just smiled.

'It's all right – I locked the briefcase!' she whispered. 'And here's the key!'

Rudy made several unsuccessful attempts to open the case, and then shrugged his shoulders. Well, too bad! After all, *he* wasn't interested in its contents! He only had to hand the whole thing over to Malik and his friends, and they would pay him for what he'd done.

He was ready to leave the room now – but he couldn't resist aiming one parting shot at his unconscious victim.

'Fancy an intelligent man being so stupid!' he told the sleeping Professor Lancing. 'I must say, scientists are a thoroughly brainless lot!'

Dick was seething with anger! He had been having difficulty controlling himself all the time Rudy was in the room, and the young man's last words were like an insult to his Uncle Quentin as well as the Professor! They really made him lose his temper. Giving way to his indignation, Dick shot out of the bathroom like a whirlwind – so suddenly that neither Julian nor George had time to stop him.

'Got you, Rudy!' he cried.

Chapter Eight

GEORGE'S UNEXPECTED ADVENTURE

Rudy stood there dumbfounded for a moment, but almost at once he pulled himself together. He slipped aside, avoiding Dick's attack, and went to the door, clutching the precious briefcase.

Dick hurtled after him – but in his haste he stumbled and fell heavily to the floor! By the time he was on his feet again, Rudy had gone.

Julian joined his brother, and between them the two boys tried turning the door handle – but the moment he was outside in the corridor Rudy had slammed the door and turned his master key in the lock. And he had left the key in the keyhole too, which meant they couldn't unlock the door from the *inside* with the Professor's room key. They were prisoners – and they could hear the young spy running off down the corridor!

But Rudy did not get very far. He turned the corner to run downstairs, and found himself face to face with Anne! Anne *had* gone down to the ground floor in the lift, but her curiosity was stronger than her fear, and it made her go back up to the first floor. She thought her brothers and her cousin might need her. So she met Rudy, with the Professor's briefcase in his hand, about to make his escape!

When she saw the young foreigner Anne thought he must have managed to carry out his original plan – and if Julian, Dick and George hadn't been able to stop him, then it was up to *her* to do something. And quickly too! But what, and how?

Anne wasn't nearly as brave and daring as George. She hated violence, and she felt very scared of Rudy. She was so small compared to him. To make matters worse, Timmy had stayed downstairs with Patrick. Anne and Timmy had found the little boy wandering round the hotel lobby all by himself.

Anne didn't stop to think about it much – she just acted on impulse. She had to stop Rudy, and instinctively she used the only thing she had with her: her pretty shepherdess's crook with its brightly coloured ribbons! She hooked her crook around the spy's legs.

Rudy was taken by surprise. He stumbled, lost

his balance, and fell head-first down the stairs — but he didn't let go of the briefcase he had stolen from the Professor.

Anne realised that she ought to have shouted for help, but she was feeling so excited and upset that she couldn't utter a sound. She leaned over the banisters and saw Rudy get up. He didn't seem to be hurt. After that she couldn't see where he went next.

'Oh dear — he's going to get away!' she thought in despair.

But Rudy's troubles weren't over yet. Before he even reached the doorway of the hotel, he saw a strange, savage monster run towards him, growling. The spy let out a cry. He couldn't believe his eyes! Rigid with terror, he watched the threatening, unknown creature. It looked like a big dog, but it had a fierce gorilla face!

Rudy couldn't know that it was only poor Timmy. Playing with the dog, little Patrick had taken off his Abominable Snowman monkey mask and put it on Timmy, who hated it! Poor thing, he couldn't even see Rudy, so he had no intention of attacking him. All Timmy was thinking of was how to get rid of that maddening mask which was blinding him.

Rudy recovered from his shock and realised it was only a dog barring his way. He walked round the 'monster' and out of the front door of the hotel.

Now he was in the street. However, he had lost precious time confronting first Dick, then Anne, and then Timmy.

And meanwhile, George was making good use of *her* time. When she saw that Rudy had got away, she quickly realised how difficult it would be to catch up with him by following him. No – what she must do was get out into the street *ahead* of him!

Leaving Julian and Dick shouting to Anne through the door to come and let them out, she turned and left Professor Lancing's room the same way as she had arrived there – through the window. She was out on the ledge in the dark again.

George had a clever plan! She knew that Malik had sent a car to the hotel to drive Rudy away with the briefcase – and Rudy would be coming out into the street any moment now. She was glad that she was invisible in the darkness wearing her cat burglar costume. She glanced down. It didn't look such a very long way from the ledge to the ground, and George was very good at gym at school. Quickly making up her mind, she dropped, and landed safely on the pavement, bending her knees in the way she had been taught. She was only a little bit shaken by the impact of landing. She straightened up and looked round. The street was deserted at this time of night. Then she looked through the glass doors and saw Rudy in the hotel lobby, facing an animal that seemed to be some kind of demon!

'Good gracious me – that's Timmy, with the monkey mask on!' said George to herself. 'Dear old Timmy – and he doesn't even know he's helping me by delaying Rudy!'

George realised she only had a few seconds in which to act, and she still didn't know just what to do. Turning round, she saw what must be the car Malik had sent, parked at the side of the road, with its engine running quietly. Yes, she couldn't have made a mistake – there was no other car waiting anywhere near.

George thought fast. The car was a foreign one, with a shiny chromium luggage rack on the back. She thought she could scramble up on it. The driver was looking at the hotel, waiting for Rudy to come out. Silent and invisible, George crept up to the car from behind and hauled herself up on the luggage rack.

Yet again she congratulated herself on choosing such a practical costume for the fancy dress party! As her clothes were black, she merged into the background crouching there on the black car, and unless you knew she was there you couldn't have seen her in the dark.

Suddenly Rudy burst out of the hotel, crossed the pavement, and flung himself into the back seat of the waiting car.

'Quick!' he told the driver. 'Let's go!'

And the car started off at once.

George clung to the luggage rack as the car gathered speed. 'Gosh!' she thought. 'I wonder what the others would say if they could see me now! I've an idea Julian would be pretty cross with me – it *is* a bit uncomfortable here. And risky too,' she added to herself, as a bump almost jolted her off her perch. 'Still, I can hardly ask Rudy to let me share his nice soft passenger seat inside, so that's just too bad! Hallo – we're outside the city now!'

A few miles farther on the car turned into a country road leading to a wood. They drove in under the cover of the trees.

George couldn't help shivering. She wasn't really regretting her bold move, but she did wonder how this adventure would turn out, and she felt a little anxious. The night air was chilly now, and she was cold in her lightweight costume. Her fingers, clutching the luggage rack, were getting frozen and numb.

'I must hang on,' she thought. 'That's the main thing.'

Luckily the journey was soon over. The car went in through a gateway and up a drive, jolting over the bumpy surface. At last it stopped outside a house. In the moonlight, George thought the place looked very sinister.

Rudy got out, and George could hear what the

driver said to him.

'You go inside. I'll stay here. I have to wait and then drive you back to Edinburgh.'

Briefcase in hand, Rudy climbed the steps to the house and pushed the door open.

Very cautiously, George got down from her perch. For a moment she hesitated. If the driver saw her she'd be in trouble! On the other hand, once well away from the car she could move about almost unseen, and the lighted window at the front of the house was very tempting. Especially as the driver of the car had his back turned to her.

Well – George always thought that fortune favours the bold, so once again she trusted to her luck!

Slowly, being very careful and bending low, she moved away from the car and over towards the lighted window. Once she reached it she cautiously straightened up until her eyes were at the level of the window-sill. To her surprise, the first person she saw inside the room wasn't Malik, but another man! He was fair-haired, with hard, bright eyes, and he was sitting at a mahogany desk. Rudy was sitting in a chair facing him. George could see both their faces.

The window had been left slightly ajar, and luckily the fair-haired man was speaking English. George strained her ears to hear what he said.

'So you got it! Excellent! However, I'd better

George clung to the luggage rack as the car gathered speed.

George strained her ears to hear what the villains were saying.

check the contents of the briefcase before I pay you.'

'You'll have to force it open, sir,' Rudy told him. 'It seems to be locked.'

Without a word, the man picked up a paperknife lying on the desk, put the point of the knife into the lock and turned it. The briefcase opened.

The spy put his hand inside – and brought out a bundle of old magazines! Rudy was watching everything he did, fascinated, and from her viewing place by the window George saw the spy's face go rigid! The man spread the worthless papers out on his desk. Now his eyes were flashing with rage!

'Are *these* the plans you were hired to steal?' he asked in a dangerous voice.

George couldn't see the expression on Rudy's face quite so well, but it was easy to guess how bewildered he must be. He turned pale. 'But . . . but . . . ' he stammered. 'The notes – the plans for the rocket! Where are they?'

'That's just what I'm asking you!' said the spy in a threatening tone. 'And if you're double-crossing us it'll be the worse for you, my boy!'

'I'm not, sir, I swear!' cried Rudy in alarm. 'I never even opened that briefcase!'

It was so obvious that poor Rudy was telling the truth, and was terrified too, that the man seemed to believe him. But it was also obvious that he was very, very angry. He abruptly got up and walked round the desk. Taking Rudy by the front of his waiter's waistcoat, he hauled him to his feet and shook him roughly.

'I haven't got time to waste on young whipper-snappers like you!' he shouted angrily. 'You've been hoodwinked, anyone can see that! And *that* means our plan has been discovered, and *you* must be the one who gave us away! Come on, admit it! You've been talking too much.'

'I haven't – truly I haven't!' cried the terrified Rudy. 'I haven't mentioned the job or Mr Malik or any of you to a living soul! I don't see how *anyone* can have guessed – unless – '

Suddenly he stopped.

'Unless what?' repeated the spy. 'Go on!'

'Well, sir – it wasn't as easy as we'd expected to steal the briefcase. Professor Lancing was asleep all right when I got into his room, but once I had the briefcase in my hands a boy who was hiding in the bathroom jumped out and tried to snatch it from me.'

The fair-haired man looked very surprised. 'A *boy*, you said?'

'Yes, sir. I know him slightly – he's staying at the holiday camp too. And now I come to think of it, it was *his* sister who delayed me when I was getting away.'

So then Rudy told the man exactly what had

happened when he tried to steal the Professor's plans. The spy listened, frowning heavily.

'Well, if I understand you correctly,' he said at last in a soft voice, 'at least two people seem to have known what you were going to do! By some miraculous means, I suppose? *I* certainly can't explain it!'

'Sir, I think that boy Dick is a spy too, like me. *He* must have stolen the Professor's plans and put these magazines in the case instead. But I arrived in the room before he could make his escape.'

'I don't think that's the explanation. If it were, he wouldn't have jumped out on you, would he? He'd just have kept quiet and waited for you to leave, and then gone himself, with the plans. Odd — very odd!' The man thought for a moment, and then went on, 'And you say his sister — the little girl dressed up as a shepherdess — seemed to be keeping watch in the corridor?'

'Yes, sir.'

'I just can't make it out. Hm . . . did anyone else see you, apart from these children?'

'No, no one at all! The lobby was empty. There isn't a receptionist at the desk after midnight, and the old night porter was busy somewhere else in the hotel.'

'Good! In that case no one can accuse you of anything, except for this boy Dick — and if *he* tries to, well, your word's as good as his! So you're in no danger.'

Rudy asked, quite humbly, 'What am I to do now, sir?'

'Nothing!' said the spy. 'Our driver will take you back to the hotel, where you'll mingle with your companions from the camp. When you get back to the camp itself you must act the same as usual. But watch those children – the ones you suspect of being spies or secret agents. And then – well, you'll get further instructions later!'

Chapter Nine

RUDY IS ON THE WATCH!

George didn't wait to hear the very end of the conversation. Moving just as cautiously as before, she crept back to the car and hauled herself up on the luggage rack again.

They drove back through the night rather fast, and the driver only stopped for a minute to let Rudy out at the Castle Hotel. George didn't dare get off her perch at the same moment. She had to wait until the car had started moving again before she jumped. She landed on the pavement with rather a bump, and was lucky not to break any bones.

Feeling a bit bruised, she made her way to the ballroom, where they were just drawing the prizes in the tombola. That was the very last thing on the programme for the party, so George had got back just in time! She saw her cousins in a corner of the room talking to Sandra, Patrick and John. She was just about to go over to them when Timmy rushed to meet *her*! His nose had told him the minute she arrived.

'Dear old Timmy – golly, I'm glad to see you! Hallo, everyone! Have you got your prizes from the tombola yet?'

Julian, Dick and Anne had been feeling very worried ever since Anne let the boys out of Professor Lancing's room and they realised that George wasn't with them any more! To make matters worse, they dared not let anyone see how worried they were. There was nothing they could do but wait anxiously in silence for George to come back. So when she did turn up at last, they felt very pleased and relieved.

'Where *have* you been, George?' asked Dick.

'Me?' said George, casually. 'Oh, I just went out for a bit of fresh air – to see if that would give me any good ideas!'

They all realised they couldn't talk freely while Sandra and John were with them.

'I'll tell you about it later – back at the camp,' George whispered to her cousins. 'Where's Rudy?'

'Over there, in his waiter's clothes – he's pretending they were for his fancy dress, of course! *He's* just come back too. In all this crowd, nobody noticed either of you was missing.'

'Well, that's a good thing,' said George.

However, Rudy was looking at the children in an odd sort of way, and when he saw them looking at *him* he quickly glanced away again.

'You don't trust us,' thought George, 'and you're quite right not to! But we have one advantage – we know what *you* are up to!'

It really was a queer situation! Rudy knew that Dick and Anne knew he was a thief and a spy. And the four cousins knew that Rudy knew that they knew! But Rudy was wondering just who Dick and Anne were. Could they be spies too, or counterspies? And Julian, Dick and Anne were surprised to see that after they'd caught Rudy in the act of trying to steal the plans he was back, boldly mixing with everyone as if nothing had happened. As for George, she couldn't wait to get back to the camp and tell the others all about her adventure!

At last all the tombola prizes had been drawn. Julian got a set of darts, Dick had a very nice musical key-ring, and George got a cookery set which she immediately gave to Anne! So Anne did very well, because her own prize was a workbasket, and she was delighted with it. After the tombola, the children all got back into the coaches, and were driven off to the camp again. Happy but sleepy, they dozed gently until they got there.

The others went to bed as soon as they were back at the camp, but the Five hurried off to meet in the boys' hut, and George told her story.

'Well!' said Julian, when she had finished. 'What a nest of spies! Malik, this fair-haired man, Rudy – obviously Rudy is going to be suspicious of us now! It's a good thing he doesn't realise just how much we know.'

Sure enough, next morning the four cousins realised that Rudy was keeping a very close watch on them, but without seeming to.

'*I* think he suspects Dick and Anne of being secret agents for this country, or some other country, but he doesn't know for certain which!' said George. 'I'm sure he suspects Julian and me too, because we're all part of the same group. But as he's still trying to work it out, all we have to do is wait and see what happens – keeping our eyes open!'

However, Julian was looking worried. 'I'm afraid we're in a bit of a mess,' he said. 'It's not so much Rudy I'm afraid of, it's the other spies. We mustn't make light of this, you know – we *are* in danger.'

Anne looked very scared.

'In danger?' she repeated in alarm. 'Oh dear! We must tell Uncle Quentin at once. George, do go and telephone him – please!'

Well, that was obviously the most sensible thing to do – and for once, even George didn't protest. This spy plot wasn't at all like the other adventures the Five had had. It was something much, much more important, and much more dangerous too.

So George went off to the telephone near the camp's office, and rang up the hotel where her parents were staying. She was quite surprised to find how relieved she felt when she heard her father's voice. Now they would get some grown-up help at last!

'Hallo, Father,' said George. 'Did you and Mother have a nice time yesterday? I tried to ring you up in the morning, but I couldn't get hold of you, and they said you were on an outing . . . oh, did you ring last night? No . . . yes, that's right, the fire only damaged a few of the huts, and the fancy dress party went ahead . . . and no, I am *not* a heroine!' she added quite fiercely. Her father had just started saying how brave she'd been to save Patrick's life! 'Oh yes, we had a lovely time at the fancy dress party last night – but listen, Father, that's not what I wanted to talk to you about. There's something very serious I want to discuss with you – could you come out here and see us?'

Just then George saw someone lurking in the corridor where the telephone was. Rudy! He was keeping at a distance, but he was close enough to hear every word she said if he was listening – and she was sure he was! George couldn't help shivering! Now she would have to be very careful what she said.

George saw that Rudy was close enough to hear every word she said.

'Look, Father,' she went on, making her voice as natural as possible, 'it's such ages since I saw you, and I miss you and Mother! Do you think you could come out here to the camp and visit me?'

Unfortunately Uncle Quentin, at the other end of the line, didn't catch the imploring note in George's apparently casual request. And he was very busy, as usual. He interrupted her.

'No, I'm afraid not,' he said. 'It's not like you to be such a baby, George. I've already wasted a lot of time going on that expedition yesterday, and I have to look at a great many papers before the next session of the conference – well, goodbye, George, and I hope the rest of your holiday is fun.'

And he hung up, leaving George at a loss – and perhaps for the first time in her life, rather scared too. With Rudy listening, she just hadn't dared to tell her father straight out what was going on.

Looking glum, she went to find her cousins, who were waiting for her near their huts.

'Well?' asked Dick eagerly.

'It's no good,' said George. And she told them what had happened. Their faces fell.

'If Rudy is going to eavesdrop on *our* telephone calls, why don't we get Sandra or John to ring up Uncle Quentin for us?' suggested Anne.

'Don't be silly!' said Dick. 'We don't want to scare the enemy off, do we? We want the police to catch those spies! So the last thing we ought to do is spread what we know about Rudy all round the camp!'

'George, why don't I write to your father?' said Julian. 'Yes – that's what I'll do!'

But George thought that wouldn't work either. 'Edinburgh may be simply swarming with secret agents,' she said. 'How do we know how many there are spying on those important scientists at the conference? Perhaps they're intercepting their letters – and they may have installed bugs too, little microphones so they can listen in on everything that's said! You know, it may be a good thing after all I didn't get a chance to tell my father all about our adventure on the telephone. That might have put us in even more danger.'

'But what can we *do*?' asked poor Anne, who was feeling terrified.

'I don't think we ought to send *any* sort of message which might be intercepted by the spies,' said George. 'I agree with Dick – we don't want to let the spies know just how much *we* know – so let's act in a perfectly innocent way, watch Rudy, and see what happens!'

Dick smiled. He knew his cousin very well – and he also knew that at heart she would be feeling really rather pleased it was all up to the Five again!

Nothing much happened for the next two days. Rudy didn't do anything unusual – so nor did the Five. Rudy certainly thought it was odd that Dick had not said anything to him about the incident at the fancy dress party. But in the end he decided that was quite reassuring. He felt more and more sure now that Dick was a spy too, working for a rival secret service, and that it was in Dick's interests as well to keep quiet.

And then, at breakfast time on the morning of the third day, a bombshell dropped. Someone had a little transistor radio in the dining-room. Julian, Dick, Anne and George were eating a very good meal of fried eggs, bacon and tomatoes when they heard a newsreader's voice.

'It has just been announced,' the newsreader was saying, 'that Professor Philip Lancing, the well-known scientist, has mysteriously disappeared from his Edinburgh hotel. It is thought that the Professor has been kidnapped. Professor Lancing was on his way to a session of the scientific conference now going on in Edinburgh. Apparently he telephoned for a taxi, and was waiting for it on the pavement outside his hotel when a large black car got there first, and two men got out and abducted the Professor in broad daylight.'

George and her cousins exchanged glances. In her mind's eye, George could see the big black car which had carried her off into the night. So now the spies had kidnapped Professor Lancing! What a cunning move!

The newsreader was going on.

'Professor Lancing was also involved in a curious incident three days ago. He had already notified the police that his briefcase, containing valuable documents, had been stolen from his room, when he found the documents in question lying about loose in the room although he had left them in the case. The briefcase itself has not been recovered.'

Sensing that Rudy was looking at them, the four cousins managed not to smile – though it was difficult! *They* knew a lot more about the stolen briefcase than the Press or the police.

They hurriedly finished their breakfast, and then, by common consent, went off to the boys' hut to discuss the situation.

Chapter Ten

A TUMBLE IN THE LAKE

'Well!' said George excitedly, when they were on their own. 'Fancy poor Professor Lancing being kidnapped!'

'And it sounds as if no one has any clue to his whereabouts,' added Julian. 'You know, I think maybe it's time we stopped waiting to see what happens next – something *has* happened next! We ought to go to the police and tell them all we know.'

'No, Ju, I don't agree,' said George. 'We can't show the police any real proof – and you can bet that Rudy won't give anything away if he's questioned. What's more, I'm pretty sure the police wouldn't believe us in the first place. It all sounds so amazing! The newspaper reporters would make a funny story out of it, and laugh at us, but all the same, *that* would tip the spies off, and then they'd probably move the Professor from the place where they're keeping him, and it would be rather difficult to get on his track again.'

'You mean you know where they're hiding him now?' asked Dick, surprised.

'Well – let's say I have a strong suspicion!' said George. 'I think we can be fairly certain that Professor Lancing is a prisoner in that house in the wood. Of course, the spies must have kidnapped him to get hold of those plans for the secret rocket – and rather than just steal his new briefcase, they may have thought the plans *might* not be inside it, so it would be more sensible to take the Professor himself too. I suppose he could write all his plans out again.'

'Yes – kidnapping him was a good idea from their point of view,' Julian agreed.

'And clever!' said Dick. 'If the actual plans were incomplete anywhere, then they could try and get the Professor to give them all the information they'd need for their country to build his rocket.'

'Do you really think the spies are keeping the Professor prisoner in that house you saw, George?' asked Anne.

'I'm practically positive! The only trouble is, I can't take you – or the police – straight there. I was so busy clinging to the luggage rack on the back of that car when I was following Rudy on the night of the party that I didn't notice just which way we went. I don't know Edinburgh at all well, and it was dark too. So I can't find my way back to the place where I saw Rudy talking to the fair-haired spy.'

George was interrupted by a low growl from Timmy. The dog suddenly hurled himself at the door and started barking frantically!

Julian looked at him in surprise. 'Hallo, old fellow – what's the matter with *you*?'

George leaped to her feet as well, flung open the door and burst out. But Timmy, who could run faster than his mistress, was already off, fast as an arrow, making for a nearby group of trees. Someone was disappearing among the trees. All George had time to see was that the figure was wearing trousers, so it could have been a boy or a girl.

'I bet it was Rudy, though,' thought George furiously. 'It can't have been anyone else. No one but Rudy would have been interested in eaves-dropping on us! And if he heard what I was saying, he knows now that *I* know rather a lot about him and his friends. Oh, what rotten luck!'

Meanwhile, Timmy had made his way into the trees. *He* knew perfectly well who his quarry was – his nose had told him. And he was determined to follow the eavesdropper and catch him!

But unfortunately, just as he was passing the trees and plunging into some bushes, a crowd of children appeared and surrounded him, with happy cries and exclamations of pleasure at seeing their favourite.

'Hallo, Timmy! Where are you going, old boy? Shake paws – say hallo!'

They were all very friendly, patting Timmy, holding his collar and making a big fuss of him. He was very popular with all the children in the camp. So when George caught up, she saw dear old Timmy surrounded by the chattering children – and there was not a sign of Rudy. If the eavesdropper really *had* been the young spy, he'd had all the time he needed to disappear without trace.

'Oh, *what* bad luck!' repeated George crossly.

* * *

And then, next day, something rather worrying happened.

There was a big diving tower anchored out in the middle of the loch – a kind of platform with diving boards at different heights on it. The weather was so warm that Andrew Saunders decided to take anyone who wanted to go out to the diving tower. They would paddle over in the camp's canoes.

George, her cousins, John, Sandra, and most of the other young people thought it was a very good idea.

There was one boy called Lennie who was always rather boastful. He went round telling everyone what a wonderful diver he was. To hear him talk, you'd think he was an Olympic medal-winner! He was even offering to give swimming lessons to anyone who wanted them. Dick decided to tease him, and maybe take him down a peg or two.

'You'd better give my cousin George some lessons, Lennie!' he suggested. 'Poor thing, she's a hopeless swimmer – she can hardly keep afloat!'

He was joking, of course. George could really swim like a fish, and was a very good diver too. She was never happier than when she was in the water.

But Lennie didn't know that, and nor did some of the others who hadn't had a chance to see George swimming. George didn't take any notice of what Dick said. Nor did Lennie, either. But Rudy had been listening too . . .

The children piled cheerfully into the canoes, and decided to have a race out to the diving tower. Once they got there they formed into groups around the diving boards.

'Now,' said Lennie, 'you just watch me do a double somersault!'

Laughing and pushing, the boys and girls crowded round to admire Lennie's performance. George was on the very edge of the platform at the bottom of the tower, a little behind the others, and like all of them she was looking up, watching Lennie climb to the diving board. Rudy was standing just behind her, but she didn't think anything of that at the time. And then – well, what exactly did happen? George was never quite sure. Was it an accident or not? Anyway, while the little girl was off her guard someone pushed her, hard, and sent her flying into the loch. No one saw her fall, because they were all still watching Lennie.

Her head struck the base of the platform quite hard as she fell, and for a moment she lost consciousness. Luckily the cold water revived her at once. Even so, she would certainly have been drowned if she hadn't been able to swim. And she could have shouted for help in vain, because Lennie was clowning away on his diving board, putting on quite a performance, while everybody else was either booing or cheering him. There was shouting and laughter, and people were making silly jokes.

You couldn't have heard a foghorn in all that din!

Poor George was absolutely bewildered by what had happened. As soon as she opened her mouth she realised it was no use calling for help – so she didn't open it again except to get her breath. Her head hurt. But she managed to swim back to the diving tower and haul herself up on the platform.

Now that she was safe her mind was working

The campers paddled out to the diving tower in canoes.

George hit her head on the platform as she tumbled into the water.

very clearly, in spite of her headache. She looked at the group of children with their backs turned to her – and she looked at Rudy too. Had he really attacked her, on purpose? Perhaps he didn't know she could swim like a fish . . .

When she came quietly up and stood beside him she saw him jump slightly, although his face showed no surprise. However, she still wasn't sure. When they all got back to the camp she told her cousins about this funny little incident.

Dick immediately jumped up and said angrily that he was going to wring Rudy's neck!

'Calm down,' Julian told his brother. 'And use your fat head! The danger's getting closer now, and we shan't do anyone any good by going for Rudy *or* by sticking our heads in the sand like ostriches. No, this time I insist – we *must* find some way of telling Uncle Quentin! We ought to have done it earlier.'

'Yes, you're right, Ju,' said George, sighing. 'We really should get in touch with my father – and since he won't come and see us, and *we* daren't write to him or ring him up, we must *go* to him. In person! I'm sure Rudy was trying to get rid of me just now, and I'm not at all keen to give him another chance.'

'Right!' said Julian. 'Now, here's what I suggest. This afternoon Andrew is organising a treasure hunt in the country outside the camp. That means we can wander off into the countryside quite casually, and no one will wonder why. I'm going to catch a bus into Edinburgh, and by this evening I'll have found Uncle Quentin and told him the whole story!'

The treasure hunt was well organised, and gave the Five just the chance they wanted. The children were divided up into several teams. They had to follow clues and find landmarks which would lead them to the 'treasure' – a bag of gold coins (chocolate ones, of course!) – hidden somewhere in the surrounding countryside. Perhaps the treasure itself wasn't really very valuable, but the hunt was going to be fun.

Shouting and laughing happily, the teams set off into the fields and woods near the loch. Julian, Dick, George and Anne began by joining in the game with the others and looking for clues – either arrows pointing the right way, or notes pinned to trees or bushes. But all the time they were making for the main road, hoping to see a bus going to Edinburgh come along.

Suddenly Anne bit back an exclamation. 'Look! Rudy!' she whispered. 'There, at that crossroads! And he's talking to somebody.'

George looked the way Anne was pointing. 'Yes – I recognise him!' she said in a low voice. 'It's the fair-haired man from the house in the wood.'

Sure enough, Rudy was talking to the spy he had

gone to meet at the house in the wood on the evening of the fancy dress party. They were both standing at the road-side in the shade of a larch tree.

'This is our chance!' whispered George. 'We must follow the fair-haired man and try to find out just where the house in the woods is!'

Yes, it certainly was a good opportunity for the Five to find their way to that house again. There was still no news of Professor Lancing, and George felt sure he must be a prisoner there – it was a fine place if you wanted to keep something or somebody hidden!

Hiding in some bushes, out of sight of Rudy and his companion, the children were wondering just *how* to follow the fair-haired man when he turned away from Rudy. Rudy crossed the road and set off along a lane. The fair-haired man stood there for a moment, looking thoughtful.

'We're in luck!' breathed Dick. 'Rudy's left the field clear for us! Come on!'

George had been thinking fast.

'See that white car parked over there? It must be the spy's! I've got an idea – he doesn't know us by sight, so we could pretend to be hitch-hikers and ask him for a lift to Edinburgh! Then, with luck, he'll drop us just before he turns off the main road to go back to the house in the woods. I assume he's going straight back there – anyway, I hope so! And that will put us on the right track!'

'How do you know he's come from the Edinburgh direction? He might have come the other way, along the road from Glasgow,' Anne said.

'But his car's parked with the bonnet pointing *away* from Edinburgh! I bet you he's going to turn it and go back the way he came. It's pretty obvious why he's driving round in that white car, too – the police will be looking out for a big black one that was used to kidnap Professor Lancing!'

'We'd better hurry!' said Julian. 'Our man's on the move!'

Sure enough, there was no time to be lost. The spy was on his way back to his car. He started the engine and turned the car, just as George had predicted. The children began to run down the slope where the bushes were and stood by the side of the main road.

Julian stepped right out into the road, so that the man had to stop. 'Oh, please, sir,' said Julian politely, 'could you possibly take us to Edinburgh? Or get us a bit closer to Edinburgh anyway! Our parents are expecting to meet us there, and we've just missed our bus.'

Chapter Eleven

THE FIVE GO HITCH-HIKING

The man looked annoyed. For a moment the children thought he was going to refuse, but then he thought better of it.

'Well, get in if you like,' he said, with a slight foreign accent, 'but I warn you I'm only going halfway to Edinburgh.'

'That's all right, sir – it'll get us closer to the city, and then we can hitch another lift,' said Dick. 'Or maybe we can walk the rest of the way.'

The boys and Anne got into the back of the car, and George sat in the front passenger seat. The man had not noticed Timmy at first, and when he did he looked cross. Thinking, like so many people, that George was a boy, he said, 'Keep tight hold of your dog, young man!'

'Don't worry, sir,' said George sunnily. 'He's not at all fierce – he'll just lie here at my feet.'

The big white car started off smoothly – George couldn't help smiling when she thought how much more comfortable this journey was than her ride on the back of the black car! 'But I'm on my way to adventure again, just as I was the other day,' she thought.

The fair-haired man drove through Leanhead village and on along the main road for about ten miles. Then he told the children that this was as far as he was going towards Edinburgh, and stopped.

The children got out of the car and thanked him, and the spy started off again at once.

'Oh, someone write down his car number, quick – have you got a pencil, Dick!' cried Anne.

'We can't *see* the number – it's all covered with mud, and you can't make out what it says!' Dick pointed out. 'It's as if he left it dirty like that on purpose.'

Julian and George were watching the car disappear. They were both hoping against hope – and their hopes were realised!

'There!' cried George excitedly. 'He *is* turning off!'

'Yes,' said Julian. 'The car's going along that track – and it seems to lead to a wood.'

'So if my suspicions are correct,' George went on, 'the spies' house must be over there. All we have to do now is explore the wood – cautiously, of course.'

'Hm,' said Julian. He looked rather downcast. 'It's a big wood, almost a forest. It'll be like looking for a needle in a haystack. If we've got to search it all, night will have fallen before we've finished – and we still may not find anything.'

'Nothing venture, nothing win!' George told him. 'Don't let's waste any more time arguing – come on! We've got *this* to help us too! I took it from the glove compartment in the car. Timmy's nose will do the job for us.'

'This' was a driving glove. George waved it triumphantly under her cousins' noses.

'It must belong to the fair-haired man,' she said. 'Once he's sniffed it Timmy will probably be able to take us straight to the house. It's worth trying, anyway!'

The children felt much more hopeful now. They liked nothing better than this kind of adventure, and dear old Timmy was always a great help! But sensible Julian decided they must take precautions.

'Just a minute!' he said, stopping George as she was about to rush off. 'There may be danger waiting for us at the spies' hide-out, so let's reduce the risk by dividing into two groups. Dick and Anne, I want you to go into Edinburgh – hitch a lift or catch a bus. Once you get there, you *must* see Uncle Quentin somehow or other.'

'Yes, it's high time we let my father know what's going on,' George agreed.

'Meanwhile George and I will look for the house in this wood,' Julian went on, 'and if we find it we'll see if we can discover whether Professor Lancing is really there. All right, everyone?'

Dick and Anne didn't much like the idea of going off without the others, but they realised that what Julian said made sense.

'Oh, all right, then,' said Dick, rather sullenly. 'Come on, Anne. There's a bus stop over there. Let's go and wait by it. If no buses come along we can always try hitching a lift in someone's car.'

'But suppose something awful happens to Julian and George while we're gone?' asked Anne anxiously.

'That's just why we *are* going,' said Dick patiently. 'To warn Uncle Quentin, in case anything *does* happen to them. So come on!'

They both went off, and Julian, George and Timmy set off after the white car.

Dick was rather worried about the other treasure hunters from the camp. If they turned up, he and Anne would have to think of some reason why they were waiting at a bus stop hoping to get to Edinburgh. And he thought that if a bus didn't come along in the next few minutes, it might be better to try and get a lift from a passing car. Dick was worried about the risks his brother and cousin

The man looked cross when he noticed Timmy.

Dick waved at the milk lorry, trying to get the driver to stop.

might be running, too. And then, when he did see Uncle Quentin, would he be able to persuade him that something must be done? Uncle Quentin was very clever, but he didn't have much common sense – he was always so wrapped up in his inventions and calculations!

'Dick, there's a car coming with two people in it,' Anne said suddenly. She had been thinking it would be safer to ask a couple for a lift than a driver on his own.

Dick stuck out his hand, and the man driving the car braked and stopped. But the woman sitting beside him looked suspiciously at the children.

'You want to get to Edinburgh, do you?' she said. 'Hm – you look rather young to be going all that way on your own. How do we know you haven't run away from somewhere?'

'But we haven't – I promise we haven't!' Dick began.

'No! We don't give lifts to strange children! Let's go on, Charles!'

And the car set off again. Anne was upset. 'Suppose nobody will give us a lift?' she wondered.

But then a truck carrying empty milk churns came along. The churns made an awful clanking noise! Dick waved as hard as he could – and the driver stopped.

'Hallo, kids! Want a lift?'

'Oh, yes, please! We've missed our bus!'

'Jump in, then, and look sharp! I'm in a hurry.'

Dick nearly said, 'So are we!' as he helped Anne up on the high step and into the truck.

Both children were very glad to reach Edinburgh. The truck driver put them down at the corner of the road leading to the Midlothian Hotel, where Aunt Fanny and Uncle Quentin were staying, and they hurried down the street, hoping very much that their aunt and uncle would be in!

Dick and Anne were just coming into the hotel lobby when they ran into a woman going out! 'Oh, Aunt Fanny!' cried Anne, seeing who it was.

'Why, hallo, Anne – hallo, Dick! Fancy seeing you here!' replied Aunt Fanny in surprise. 'What are you doing in Edinburgh? You were lucky to find me – your uncle's at his conference, and I was just going out to do some shopping. What's the matter? And where are George and Julian? Oh, my goodness, I do hope nothing has happened to them!'

Aunt Fanny was looking worried – she knew how reckless George could be! But Dick soon reassured her.

'No, nothing like that!' he said. 'But we *must* talk to Uncle Quentin. It's urgent! It – it's to do with a spy plot and Professor Lancing, and that's why George and Julian sent us here to find you!'

Astonished, Aunt Fanny looked at her nephew in silence for a moment or so – and then, realising that he wasn't joking, she said, 'Well, all right, let's go up to my room. Tell me what it's all about, and then I'll telephone your uncle.'

As it happened Aunt Fanny had a lot of trouble getting through to the conference centre, and when at last she did, a laboratory technician told her it was more than his job was worth to interrupt the scientists. But if Aunt Fanny didn't mind coming herself, he said, *she* could take the responsibility of disturbing her husband!

Aunt Fanny was not very pleased, but she decided to go. 'Come with me, children,' she told Dick and Anne. 'We'll take a taxi to the conference centre.'

They found a taxi at the taxi rank close to the hotel – and very soon the three of them had reached the building where the scientific conference was going on. But Aunt Fanny had to answer a lot of questions and do a good deal of arguing before at last she was allowed in! 'Wait here,' she told the children. 'I'll soon be back with your uncle – I hope!'

However, Dick and Anne had been sitting in the waiting-room, feeling very impatient, for what seemed like ages when someone they hadn't expected at all arrived. Rudy! At first they couldn't believe their eyes, but it was Rudy all right. Eyes down, the young spy was looking as if he were deep in thought as he came into the waiting-room.

Before he had time to spot Anne and Dick, Dick got up, pulling his sister along with him, and they went through a door marked CLOAKROOM.

'We don't want him to know we're here,' he whispered to Anne. 'That would make him suspicious – and then he would phone his employers to warn them to be on their guard. I wonder why he's here?'

But Dick was interrupted. The cloakroom door opened – and Rudy came in. When he saw the children he stopped short in astonishment.

Then he smiled, spitefully! He took a step backwards – but Dick wasn't going to let him get away a second time. He knew that it was important to put Rudy out of action. With one bound he jumped at him, caught him off balance and knocked him down. It was all over in a flash!

Rudy's head hit the floor, and he lost consciousness. Dick seized his opportunity to tie Rudy up with his own belt and gag him with a handkerchief.

'Quick, Anne – help me get him inside this broom cupboard! That'll dispose of *him* – and leave us free to act.'

To make extra sure, Dick tied him up even more firmly with some dusters and put a bucket over his head. Then he locked the cupboard, and put the key in his pocket. Satisfied with the job he had done, he went back to the waiting-room, and Anne followed him.

But while Dick and Anne were doing their best to get help from Uncle Quentin, warn the police and get the spies caught, what had become of Julian, George and Timmy?

Chapter Twelve

THE FIVE TO THE RESCUE

Well, George and Julian hadn't been wasting their time.

First of all, they hurried down the road to the track where the spy's white car had turned in. They walked along the track for quite a long time. There was open country on both sides of it, and that rather bothered Julian.

'If the spies can watch this track from the windows of their house,' he said to his cousin, 'they can't help seeing us coming!'

'Don't worry,' said George, 'We're still some way from the wood, and I remember we seemed to drive for quite a time the other night before we got to the house in the middle of it. We're not near the place yet.'

Julian was glad of that, and the two cousins went

on walking along the track as fast as they could.

Timmy was the only one who really enjoyed such a long walk on a hot day like this! But at last the children reached the cool shade of the wood.

'Phew!' breathed George. 'This is better!'

'Yes!' said Julian, 'but we must be on the alert now. We're coming to the dangerous part!'

'Timmy!' called George. 'Now's your chance to show us how clever you are, old boy! Here, sniff this glove – now find its owner!'

Running up and wagging his tail, Timmy obediently sniffed the glove. Then he raced forward. The children followed him until they reached a place where the track forked.

George hesitated here – but clever Timmy knew where he was going! Without even stopping, he went off along the path to the right.

'Good dog, Timmy!' said Julian admiringly. 'If we didn't have him with us we wouldn't have had the faintest idea which way to go. What a good tracker dog he is!'

'Yes, but that's not surprising. He *is* one of the Five, after all!' said George, who was really very proud of her dog.

The two cousins walked slowly on through the trees. Now and then they called to Timmy in a low voice, and gave him the fair-haired man's glove to sniff again, just to encourage him in his search.

Suddenly George slowed down even more.

'I think we're getting close now,' she told Julian in a whisper. 'I seem to remember crossing a clearing very like this one the other day.'

All at once she stopped dead, and squeezed her cousin's arm.

'Look!' she breathed. 'There's the house!'

Julian stopped too. Looking through the tree trunks, he saw a large white house. It had a garden all round it, and there was a tall fence round the garden, with a gate in it.

'Gosh – you didn't tell me it was such a fortress of a place!' said Julian. 'We'll never get in there!'

'I suppose you're right,' said George, ruefully. 'Now I see it in daylight, I can tell that getting in *will* be difficult. But not impossible!'

'George, let's go back the way we came,' said Julian. 'We've found the spies' hideout, and that's the main thing. The rest will be up to the police.'

But George didn't agree. Now that she was actually on the spot she didn't want to go tamely back again! 'No,' she said. 'Since we're here, we can at least see whether Professor Lancing really *is* being kept prisoner in the house. Give me a leg up, Julian! I'm going to climb the fence and have a look round.'

'You're mad! You're not going to walk straight into the lion's den, are you?'

'No, of course not! I'll be very careful, I promise.'

But Julian did his best to stop George doing something so dangerous.

'Do stop and think, George! It's far too risky! That fence may be electrified – or connected up to burglar alarms in the house. Or there may be mantraps inside the garden. Don't go in, George – please! And if you do, you needn't count on *me* to help you!'

'All right then, I'll manage without you!' said George angrily.

She was already making for the fence when they heard the sound of an engine! A car was coming. The two cousins took shelter behind a bramble bush, making Timmy go with them.

They were only just in time. A van came bumping along the path and stopped at the garden gate. The driver got out to open the gate. He was on his own, and there were two crates in the back of the van.

On impulse, George came to a decision. Leaving poor Julian behind, she took advantage of the moment when the driver's back was turned to them to scurry towards the van, bending over. She hauled herself up into the back of the van and hid behind one of the crates.

Timmy wanted to follow his mistress, and Julian had to hold him back. The boy was horrified! Had George any idea of the danger she was running into? Badly worried, but helpless to do anything, he saw the driver get back behind the wheel and go through the gateway. Then he stopped and got out again to close the gates. George was in enemy territory!

What would happen now? Craning his neck, Julian stared through the brambles.

But George had no intention of going any farther in the van. She jumped down and went to hide behind one of the clumps of shrubs beside the drive. Phew! Her plan had worked!

Now to find out whether or not Professor Lancing was really a prisoner here!

The van set off towards the house. George hadn't really thought out the next part of her plan of action. First she wanted to get close to the house. After that, she'd see. She was trusting to luck – and her luck seldom let her down. Though Julian, in his hiding place, didn't feel nearly so happy about it!

For the time being, however, luck did seem to be on the brave girl's side. She made her way from bush to bush, and got quite close to the house. She was soon near enough to the driver to hear him talking in a loud voice as he unloaded his crates.

'I suppose you realise I've made this dangerous journey specially for you?' he was saying. 'Yes – here's all the stuff you need to make a working model of your rocket. Oh yes, they've told me all about it – and they say *you* say you'll refuse to make it. But you don't know the boss! He knows how to make people work!'

Startled, George realised that the man was not talking to himself, as she had thought at first. But where was his companion? There was no one in sight, and she couldn't even hear another voice. However, she knew he must be talking to Professor Lancing!

The driver fell silent and finished unloading his crates. Then he carried them into the house. Perhaps he was going to open them indoors. George began cautiously advancing once again.

After she had gone a little way she stopped, and looked round her with curiosity. She was beside the van now – but still she couldn't see anyone or anything, except an old well with a lid over it.

However, George's sharp, inquisitive eyes spotted a ventilator shaft with an opening at ground level. Why would a well have a ventilator shaft? George thought she knew the answer. This well was a kind of secret prison, hidden away from the house itself. There must be some sort of device to let people talk to the prisoner from outside.

And thanks to this well, the spies weren't running many risks. Even if the children *did* manage to persuade the police to raid the house, their search wouldn't reveal anything. The prisoner would not be discovered!

George didn't hesitate for a moment. If she was

right, it was up to *her* to rescue Professor Lancing!

She went over to the well. 'Professor!' she said in a low voice. 'Are you down there? I'm George Kirrin – Quentin Kirrin's daughter. If you can hear me, please try to reply!'

Much to her delight, a faint but audible whisper answered her.

'Yes! Yes, I'm here, at the bottom of the well! I'm shouting as loud as I can – can you hear me?'

'Yes, I can hear you quite all right, though your voice only sounds like a whisper,' George told him. 'Hang on, Professor! I'm going to get you out!'

But George had spoken rather too soon. She tried moving the lid off the well, but it was no good. It wouldn't budge! And then, when she was least expecting it, disaster struck!

A hand came down on her shoulder, and she heard the fair-haired man's voice.

'Well, well, well – if it isn't my young friend the hitch-hiker!'

The man pressed a button hidden between two stones beside the well – and the circular lid slid smoothly aside, revealing the top rungs of an iron ladder.

'Sorry, my lad, but curiosity killed the cat, you know!' said the spy harshly. 'So down you go!'

When George didn't move, he took her roughly by the elbow – but almost at once he let go of her again, howling in pain. Timmy had just leapt on him and got him by the ankle!

Julian was so worried that *he* had decided to climb the fence himself, even though he hadn't wanted George to go over. As for Timmy, he had managed to wriggle between two of the railings. With his nose to the ground, the dog was quick to pick up his little mistress's scent – and he was ready to fight to the death to defend her, if need be!

'You brute!' snarled the fair-haired man, struggling with the dog.

Leaning over the side of the well, George called down, 'Quick, Professor Lancing! Climb up if you can – you can get out now!'

Professor Lancing had been kicking his heels down in the underground room fitted up as a prison at the bottom of the well, and she didn't have to ask him twice! The lid of the well couldn't be moved except from outside, so he had not been tied up in his prison. And he started the long climb up. When he came out of the well, he found himself in the middle of a dramatic scene.

Julian, George, Timmy and the fair-haired man were all tangled in a confused heap on the lawn! Professor Lancing, seeing what was going on, tried to come to the aid of his unexpected rescuers. But he was just too late! The spy managed to get a hand free, pulled a whistle out of his pocket and put it to his lips.

Almost at once, five or six men came running up.

When Professor Lancing came out of the well, he found himself in the middle of a dramatic scene.

138

They must have heard the whistle from inside the house.

George, Julian and the Professor knew it was no use resisting any longer. They couldn't hope to fight so many men – one of them was already holding Timmy by the collar and half-strangling him.

'Brute!' the fair-haired man repeated, looking at Timmy. 'You just wait – you'll be sorry for this!'

And one of the men was aiming a pistol at poor Timmy. He looked as if he was about to fire it. George immediately got in front of her dog.

'Don't you *dare* touch Timmy!' she said defiantly. 'He's worth a thousand times more than you are!'

'Now, move aside, lad, or – '

But the spy never finished what he was saying. A voice came from the bushes beside the gravel drive.

'Drop that gun and put your hands up! Right – hands up, all of you! Professor, will you and the children move aside?'

Professor Lancing pulled George and Julian away from the lawn, and Timmy followed them. A crowd of policemen surged forward out of the bushes!

George shouted for joy as she saw her father and Dick and Anne running towards her.

'Oh, Father, I'm so pleased to see you!' she cried. 'You arrived just in time!'

'We've been searching the whole wood to find you – whatever have you got mixed up in *now*?' growled Uncle Quentin, trying to sound cross, though really he was as delighted as George!

Professor Lancing interrupted.

'Don't be angry with her, Kirrin!' he said. 'She's a very brave girl! She saved me *and* my rocket! There – look at that!'

Beaming with pleasure, the four cousins saw the fair-haired man and his accomplices being led past in handcuffs. George recognised Malik as they went by.

'A pity Rudy's not there too,' muttered Julian. 'They need him too, to round things off!'

'Don't worry!' said Dick, laughing. 'The police picked *him* up from his broom cupboard!'

'Broom cupboard? What on earth do you mean?' asked his puzzled brother.

'Tell you later!'

Back at the camp by Loch Lean that evening, everyone was congratulating the Five on their daring adventure! As for Timmy, he had a lovely time, with so many people fussing over him!

'You know,' George told her cousins during the camp-fire party being held in honour of the Five, 'I've really enjoyed staying in Scotland! If we hadn't had this little adventure, I think I might have found the summer holidays just a bit dull after all!'

If you have enjoyed this book here are some more adventures that you might like to read, also available from Knight Books:

THE FAMOUS FIVE AND THE STATELY HOMES GANG

The Five are pleased to be spending another holiday at Kirrin Cottage, the scene of many of their adventures. And this holiday proves to be as exciting as the others, from the moment they set off on their shiny new bicycles!

THE FAMOUS FIVE VERSUS THE BLACK MASK

A Mediterranean cruise on the liner *North Wind* is an exciting prospect for the Five and their friend Tinker.

Then a series of thefts confirms a rumour that the famous international criminal, the Black Mask, is on board! Who, out of all the innocent-looking passengers, can the thief be? The children are determined to find out before the end of the holiday!

KNIGHT BOOKS

THE FAMOUS FIVE AND THE
BLUE BEAR MYSTERY

Back at Kirrin for Christmas, the Five find some
very strange things are happening in the town.
First someone steals Dr Thompson's Christmas
tree, and then there is a peculiar theft at the Kirrin
Stores. After a strange lady offers to buy Anne's
teddy bear, the Five decide to investigate.

KNIGHT BOOKS

Other adventures of the Famous Five, told by Claude Voilier and translated by Anthea Bell, include:

THE FAMOUS FIVE AND THE
INCA GOD
THE FAMOUS FIVE AND THE
CAVALIER'S TREASURE
THE FAMOUS FIVE AND THE
STRANGE LEGACY
THE FAMOUS FIVE AND THE
SECRET OF THE CAVES

KNIGHT BOOKS